The Darkness
And The Dawn

Susan Feldhake's *Enduring Faith Series*

1. In Love's Own Time
2. Seasons of the Heart
3. For Ever and Ever
4. Hope for the Morrow
5. From This Day Forward
6. Joy in the Morning
7. Serenity in the Storm
8. The Darkness and the Dawn

ENDURING FAITH SERIES
8

The Darkness And The Dawn

SUSAN FELDHAKE

ZondervanPublishingHouse
Grand Rapids, Michigan

The Darkness and the Dawn
Copyright © 1996 by Susan Feldhake

Requests for information should be addressed to:

▆ZondervanPublishingHouse
Grand Rapids, Michigan 49530

Library of Congress Cataloging-in-Publication Data

Feldhake, Susan C.
   The darkness and the dawn / Susan Feldhake.
      p.   cm. — (Enduring faith ; bk. 8)
   ISBN: 0-310-20262-0
   I. Title. II. Series: Feldhake, Susan C. Enduring faith series ; bk. 8.
PS3556.E4575D37 1996
813'.54—dc 20   96-3378
                                                     CIP

Edited by Robin Schmitt

Printed in the United States of America

96 97 98 99 00 01 02 /❖ DH/ 10 9 8 7 6 5 4 3 2 1

chapter
1

"OH . . . AIN'T it a beautiful day?!" Lizzie Mathews exuberantly cried when she stepped from the veranda overhang of the Grant Hotel and surveyed the landscape.

A gentle midmorning breeze, fresh with the tang of pine scent, riffled her hair as sunlight slanted across her cheeks, which had filled out and regained the blush of good health after a long season of draining illness.

"Just gorgeous, Liz," her husband, Brad, agreed.

"We couldn't have received a more perfect day iffen we'd been able to custom order one out o' a mail-order catalog!" Lester Childers, Lizzie's son, added.

"Ayuh," Joy, Lester's wife, a white woman who'd been raised among the Chippewa and who was bloomingly in the family way, affirmed.

"It's been years since I've seen him," Marissa Wheeler Wellingham wistfully sighed. "He'll pro'bly look the same as always, I reckon. Regardless, that man'll be a sight for sore eyes after what we've all been through!"

Dr. Marc Wellingham regarded his pretty wife, who held their son, Curtis Alton. The child wrapped his fingers in his mother's long hair, the better to hang on and steady himself in her arms. "Surely you've changed, darling," Marc said, "since he's seen you."

7

"No doubt Molly's changed more," Luke Masterson, Molly's husband, said as he slid his arm around his wife's slim shoulder while he nestled their daughter, Susannah, in his other arm. "I watched Molly change—like a flower blooming—after she came to Williams."

"There were times I wondered whether we'd ever see that feller alive again!" Lizzie said. "I'd about give up hope."

"It's going to be a grand reunion!" Brad said.

"An answer to prayer!" Molly agreed.

Lizzie, dressed in her Sunday best—as was Brad, who gallantly claimed her arm—led the way toward the Canadian National Railroad depot, like a grand marshal in a small-town parade.

"All that's missin' is a brass band!" Lester joked.

"I think I just heard the train a-comin'!" Brad announced. "Iffen I did—must be about at what's left o' Cedar Spur after the Big Fire."

Lester cocked his head, listening intently. Between soft gusts of breeze, he believed he heard a faint *whoo-whoo!* as the engineer hauled on the cord, releasing a shriek of steam from the train's whistle.

"Sure enough! Train's coming!" Luke assured.

"I feel like a kid waitin' on Christmas morn," Lizzie admitted. "I'm just plumb excited! I get first hug!"

"Of course. You've more right'n anyone," Brad said, patting her elbow, grinning down at her.

"What a welcoming committee we present," Lizzie said, looking around her with beaming approval. "Won't be no doubt in his mind about how glad we are to see him alive 'n well, will there?"

"It appears fam'bly ain't the only ones waitin' on him," Lester said. "Some of our friends are showin' up for the occasion, too!"

"I reckon it's 'cause they know that someone dear to us'll soon be dear to them too!" Lizzie pointed out.

"Even though he's seen some o' this big ol' world and the big city lights since he hied away from the Salt Creek community, he cain't help but be impressed by his reception!"

"I'm looking forward to meeting him," Joy said, smiling shyly. "I feel in some ways like I already know him."

"No doubt he'll feel the same about you," Brad assured.

"I have an idea! Do you think that maybe we should hide and let him think no one's here to meet him? That we've forgotten when he was to arrive? And then when he's looking confused and perplexed and wondering if he's welcome after all—we could jump out and shout, 'SURPRISE!'"

Molly, the more sedate and sensitive of the adult Wheeler twins, frowned. "That'd be plumb mean, 'Rissa!" she objected. "He may have hesitancies enough about showing up here, without giving him cause to have doubts fermenting in his mind."

"We'll just stand here on the siding," Lizzie said, settling it once and for all, "and greet him big as you please."

"Lester, y'all got that welcome banner ready to unfurl?" Brad inquired.

"Sure do! Y'can count on Joy 'n me!"

"When I catch sight of him in the doorway of the train coach, I'll say, 'One . . . two . . . three,' and then we'll all holler out welcoming greetings at once," Lizzie stipulated.

The chug and clatter of the approaching CNR train grew louder, and soot and sparks plumed upward from the squatty smokestack.

The whistle shrilled, cleaving the pine-scented air as the engine cleared the crossing just a half mile east of the village.

Lizzie covered her ears as the ground trembled beneath the rumbling weight of the train. With a huffing chug and jolting clank, steel clashed against steel as the brakeman threw the lever.

Moments later the engine rolled to a halt precisely in front of the clapboard depot. Soon passengers began to straggle off the train. The conductor offered womenfolk a steadying hand.

"I think I just caught a glimpse o' him!" Lizzie cried. "He's about to show up in the doorway! Everyone get set....One ... two ... THREE!"

"WELCOME TO WILLIAMS, LEMONT GARTNER!" they cried out as Lester and Joy unfurled a lettered banner—made out of old hotel dishtowels sewn together—that read the same.

For a moment, the old man seemed to almost fall backward in amazement. Then he wrestled ahead with his burden of possessions. A grin was frozen on Lem's face, as if he were intent on rigidly smiling, for fear that if he relaxed, he'd burst into happy tears at the very sight of them all.

Lizzie flew into his arms, almost knocking him over, as Brad stepped forward to relieve him of a bundle or two.

"Lem! It's so good to see you!" Lizzie cried, soundly bussing his cheeks.

"It's grand to be here, Miss Lizzie," he said. "And Brad! Howdy do, my good fellow!"

"You're lookin' great," Brad said, enthusiastically pumping the hand that Lemont had offered even as Lizzie continued to hug him.

"Lizzie Mathews! Don't hog Grandpa Lem all to yourself!" Marissa Wellingham merrily complained, transferring little Curt to her husband's arms.

Lemont turned toward her as she spoke. His eyes widened, he chuckled at the sight of her, and he wiped a skim of happy tears from his cheeks as the town physician's wife gave him a big hug.

"Little Marissa! . . ." Lem said, shaking his head in delighted awe at the changes wrought in her. When he'd seen her last, she'd been a coltishly pretty, defiant, rebellious spitfire of a girl. Now she was a pearl of a woman....

"Not so little anymore," Marissa corrected.

"I should say you're not!" Lem agreed. "All growed up you are, and the mother of a fine son!" He reached out to tug the little boy's pinkie finger.

Marissa didn't settle for just that. She scooped Curt from Marc's arms and thrust him at Lemont.

"Time to get to know your Grandpa Lem, Son," Marissa said.

Gingerly Lem held the toddler, who didn't cry but looked from his mother to his father to assure himself that they remained nearby.

"Grandpa Lem . . .," the retired farmer repeated, savoring the words as he held the child. "I like the sound of that!"

"I should hope you do," Molly Masterson good-naturedly chided as she stepped forward to present herself and her husband and their tiny daughter.

"Grandpa Lem—meet our little Sarah Nell!"

" . . . Oh!" Lem said as Molly pulled back a corner of the bunting blanket to reveal her features, which were placid and peaceful in her sleep. "Ain't she a treasure?!"

"As girlish as li'l Curt appears to be all boy, is what I say," Lizzie pointed out.

Luke extricated their daughter from Molly's arms so she was freed to hug the neighbor man she'd known for all of her days.

"Molly girl . . . Molly girl!. . .," Lemont crooned, almost overcome.

Molly was misty-eyed, too. "It's so good to see you. Surrounded by so many familiar faces, I hadn't realized exactly how homesick I've become for those we left behind."

"Well, they're still there . . .'cept for . . ."

Lemont's voice trailed off. Even with the name unspoken,

everyone's thoughts were suddenly drawn to Thad Childers. And, of course, to Harmony LeFave.

"Lem, I thought you'd be travelin' light," Lester quickly said, in what seemed a desperate bid to keep the happy reunion from becoming morose.

"Numerically, he probably is," Brad chimed in to assist Lester's efforts. "Only two bags, count 'em up! But the pair is plumb weighty!"

"What've you got in there, Lem? Rocks?!" Lester joshed.

"A few changes of clothes 'n a few doodads in the one valise. In the other, ain't rocks—simply good ol' central Illinois, clay-heavy dirt! Thought you might appreciate a bit o' the old home place."

"Dirt?!" Lizzie gasped.

"Well, and whatever's in the dirt."

"Y'know, Liz has been sickly in the not too distant past, neighbor. She still confuses purty easy if you toy with her mind," Brad said, winking broadly.

"I brought you somethin' from home, Miss Lizzie. For you!" he said, thrusting the ancient, bulging suitcase toward her.

"For me?"

"Yessirree!"

Brad reached out to assist her with the load.

"What can it be?" Lizzie said.

"Look inside and see!"

Lizzie unlatched the leather straps from metal buckles. Inside were neatly twined-up balls of burlap, carefully labeled.

"Heavens!" she cried, her hands flying to her cheeks in surprise.

"It's rose shoots. A whole passle of 'em."

"And not just any shoots!" Lizzie cried with overwhelming understanding. "Oh, I hope 'n pray they're hardy enough to survive in these parts!"

"We can always straw 'em up real good, darlin', and wrap them in canvas come the cold months," Brad suggested.

Lizzie let out a happy wail and once more flung herself into Lemont's arms. "You're a kind and thoughtful gent, you are, Lemont Gartner," she cried. "Why, wearin' yourself to a nubbin', lugging around such a dead weight on account o' me. I can't thank you enough, Lem!"

"Seein' your joy is thanks enough, Miss Lizzie. They're all there and labeled securely with India ink on cloth so's there'll be no confusion."

Lizzie looked at the labels and regarded the rose bushes, and her thoughts spanned back over the years, as the names represented a litany of loved ones who'd passed on, returned to the earth, but had wondrous rose bushes to mark their final resting sites.

Sue Ellen . . . Harmon . . . Pa . . . Ma . . . Jeremiah . . . Maylon . . . Alton . . . Miss Abby. . . . She would add their shoots to the newly transplanted one from Harmony's gravesite at Billy LeFave's cabin at the lake.

"What a bower of roses I'll have," Lizzie whispered, her voice tremulous with scarcely pent tears. "A bush to create a garden of memories for each dear departed loved one's restin' place." Lizzie swallowed hard. "'Cept for Thad. . . ."

Silence spiraled out, settling over the group like a pall.

"That can't be helped," Brad said in a pained whisper and quickly slipped his arm around Lizzie.

"Between Molly and Lizzie, Williams might end up being the rose capital of the northland," Luke Masterson said, trying to inject a bit of levity into their mood.

Lizzie refused to let them coddle her.

"It'll be purty," she said. "And I pray the Lord that Thad's final restin' place at least has dandylions to beautify it!"

Lester drew in a quick breath. "They'd be plumb suitable. He liked 'em."

"Liked butter too," Lizzie said, "Just like a dandylion under his chin said that he would."

"That was just superstition. No one in his right mind could resist butter by your hand, Liz Mathews."

"Especially when it was rendered into sugar cookies!" Lester added.

"Speakin' o' which, there's a platter of 'em fresh-frosted and a pot o' coffee on the range. Let's hie on back to the hotel, kick back and relax for a bit, enjoy the refreshments, and get a chance to catch up a bit before the noon business begins!"

"Hope you've got a pot full of vittles," Sven Larson, one of the Meloney Brothers' lumberjacks, warned as he came up to greet Lem. "There's a lot of us counting on those celebration cookies, who'll stay on to be paying customers come noon!"

"Glad to have y'all!" Lizzie said, casting a welcoming smile of invitation to all who'd clustered at the depot to take in the day's excitement.

When they all arrived at the Grant Hotel, Lester rushed ahead to hold the door for the others.

"This here's your new home, Lem," Brad said, "for as long as you're wantin' to stay here. And don't be in any hurry to depart."

"I ain't," Lem assured. "Fact is, I only bought a one-way ticket!"

Lizzie seemed to brighten over that knowledge.

"Well, after many seasons of tragedy and tribulation, that's the best news I've received in a long, long time!"

chapter
2

New Orleans, Louisiana

SUNLIGHT STREAMED THROUGH the stained-glass windows of the church as the worship service drew to a close. The notes from the pipe organ drifted off to infinity as Nanette Kelly's singing, which had been sweet and clear as a flute, with her lower register mellow as sun-warmed honey, ended.

She lowered her head in a humble gesture and also in order that she might squeeze her eyes against the quick sting of tears when she realized that it'd be the last time she would sing before her beloved friends in the close-knit congregation. At least the last time for a long, long while.

The church was in awed silence, and Nanette realized that they had been no less inspired by her rendition than she, and she was aware that she'd given the song "Amazing Grace" the best and most moving performance of her Christian life.

The pastor proceeded into the benediction.

As they filed toward the street following the service's conclusion, with people stopping to pass the time over a bit of conversation, word quickly spread that a surprise farewell party for Nanette had been secretly planned. Womenfolk of the church were hastily setting plates of delicacies, which had been hidden from view earlier, onto long tables underneath the magnolia trees that landscaped the church property.

Serving as a centerpiece in the midst of the platters of culinary treats was a sapling that served as a money tree, to which were affixed bills and cheerfully bright and swaying coins.

"For you, Nanette," the pastor said, "to help finance you as you do the Lord's work and answer his call to minister in word and song."

Nanette was caught off guard. "I can't thank you enough! You've already done so much by arranging with various churches for me to appear as a guest at their services."

"Granted, that I did," the pastor agreed, "but the money tree is from your church family. The idea and thanks go to your brothers and sisters in Christ who are supporting you with funds as they'll remember you in steadfast prayer."

Nanette had not expected a party, and now she realized why Mrs. Poindexter had been tippy-toeing around, talking in hushed whispers, and periodically having a dreamy smile on her features even when there was nothing in their immediate environment that should seem to have the elderly owner of the boardinghouse scarcely able to contain her grins.

"I'm going to miss each and every one of you," Nanette said as she exchanged hugs, handshakes, and words of departure while the congregation's members began to take their leave.

"Stay in touch, dear," many an elderly dowager admonished.

"I will!" Nanette said.

"She's given me her itinerary," Mrs. Poindexter said. "We can mail her letters of news and encouragement, and she can receive them in care of the churches where she'll be appearing. And general delivery at the post office in a few cities along the way."

"Wonderful!"

"You may be out of sight, Nan, but you'll always be in our hearts and prayers."

"I don't know when it'll be, but someday I'll return for a visit, Lord willing. You're the only family I have."

"You've got a wonderful family waiting to get to know you as you meet our brothers and sisters in Christ in the course of your travels."

"Strange, I find myself excited—yet also afraid. Mrs. Poindexter, who'd have ever imagined it: me, Nanette Kelly, witnessing and singing for the Lord Jesus Christ! Why, there was a time in my life when his name was used only as an oath to express fury or disgust."

"It's been that way for different folks, honey. You're not alone in your reversals."

"I—I know that I've got gifts, God-given gifts—a gift for singing that I used to squander in saloons and a gift for conversation that onct upon a time I used for convincing people of my earnestness as my brother and I sought to hoodwink them. No doubt there are people who knew the old Nanette Kelly who'd laugh themselves faint-headed to hear me now. I fear some of them would assume that I was a hypocrite and that freewill offerings were just another scam to relieve folks of their funds."

"Don't you trouble your head and heart about that, girl," Mrs. Poindexter ordered. "The Lord calls whom he will—and when you hear the call, it's best to answer it quickly and willingly. The Lord's path, even when it seems uphill and difficult, is actually the smoothest course through life. Trust in him to guide your life and your ministry, and you'll never be led wrong. He'll take you places that you might've dreamed of but could've never attained on your own, no matter how hard you tried."

That afternoon, following a sumptuous dinner in which Mrs. Poindexter outdid herself, there was a steady stream of callers who'd come by the huge boardinghouse to give Nanette a last farewell.

She'd planned to see her own way to the pier in order to board the *River Queen* for its northern journey but was relieved when the pastor and his wife insisted that they would consider it an honor to transport Nanette—and Mrs. Poindexter—to the steamship so they could have a final farewell.

"I love you all!" Nanette said the next morning at the dock, exchanging hug after hug with Mrs. Poindexter and the pastor's wife, as they were all caught in a warp between the sadness of a departure and the excitement realized in Nanette's setting out on a special walk in her Christian life.

"Write soon!" Mrs. Poindexter cried out, waving her hanky as the steamship drifted away from its mooring and slowly moved toward the channel.

"I will!" Nanette promised. "Very likely I'll begin penning correspondence while I'm resting in my quarters this evening."

The recent weeks as she'd made her plans to go forward in the world to minister in word and song had been busy ones for Nanette. There'd been so many details to attend to and tasks to perform before she could depart.

With the voyage suddenly undertaken and her dream realized, it was as if the exhaustion that had dogged her during long and arduous days of late had finally caught up with her. She'd scarcely settled into her quarters, was going to read from the Good Book for a while, when drowsiness captured her and she floated off to sleep.

It was late afternoon before she awakened, feeling logy from the midday nap in the sultry southern-bayou environment, and began to freshen up for dinner.

When Nanette was shown to her table, she was grateful that her dinner partners were elderly and simple folk who didn't count on her for artful and vivacious conversation, for she was steeped in her own thoughts, plans, and dreams.

She'd once been transported south along the Mississippi River, and now as the steamboat paddled northward, it was as if her entire perspective had been changed. But then she realized that it had, because now she was viewing the world through the eyes of a committed Christian, and before . . . she hadn't.

A lot has happened, she mused as she let herself into her cabin after a leisurely stroll on the deck prior to retiring.

And she had learned tremendous lessons in living. Now she could see the plan that the Lord had made for her life even years before she was to hear of him and ask him into her heart. Bad things had happened to her, good things, too, and they all compiled to weave together the fabric of her life as it was threaded together with others' existences to create a glorious tapestry of God's creation.

Redwing, Minnesota

Hurdy-gurdy music rent the air as the shrilling circus calliope screamed out merrily discordant tunes to better assist carnival-goers in maintaining cheerful, money-spending, adventure-seeking outlooks.

"Step right up, ladies and gentlemen," the carny barker cried, "and sit right down! The show's about to begin! See Mr. Tiny, the world's smallest man, who is only an amazing nineteen inches tall! See him seated on the lap of Lulabelle, the circus fat lady, who last weighed in at an astounding seven hundred pounds!"

The steps of the passersby slowed, even in the wilting heat that was scarcely diluted by the light wind wafting in on the Mississippi River, which meandered south of Minneapolis–St. Paul to pass by Redwing, where a reform school for boys and a work boot factory were housed. At present, Redwing was home, for the weekend, to a carnival that had sprung up at the edge of town.

"Seeing is believing!" the carny barker continued his patter, knowing that if people slowed to listen, the chance that he could cajole them past the ticket attendant and inside the exposition tent greatly increased.

"Step right up, folks, sit down, rest your feet, and ease back and experience sights that your neighbors 'n kinfolk'll be talking about for days and weeks to come. Don't deny yourselves this opportunity, my good people, to be in the know along with all o' your friends and family. Give your young'uns an ed-u-ca-tional opportunity of a lifetime! See in real life what otherwise you might only get to look at in an en-cy-clo-pedia!"

Seventeen-year-old Lolly Ravachek sat in a tent to the rear of where the elaborately dressed, powdered, polished, and pomaded barker had positioned himself to accost the milling crowds.

The freak-show tent was a larger edifice than what Lolly's family owned, but it took little space to house a fortune-teller's table. Inside the Ravachek tent it was dim, hot, stuffy, and the atmosphere was made even more wretched by the flaring of myriad stubby candles flickering in the musty, mildewy, canvas-constructed grotto.

"Know the future—today!" Anton Ravachek, Lolly's father, urged persuasively, challenging the freak-show barker for customers with change in their pockets and a free-spending carnival mood that would certainly end as soon as the spell was broken and they departed the make-believe world of the circus to face the all too glaring realities of their workaday lives.

"Readings are quick! Reliable! Accurate! Illuminating! Our fortune-tellers aren't fakes or frauds, nosirree! Through powers that only they possess and use, they can dazzle you with their insights and information. They can reveal the past, talk

about the present, and warn you of your future as it's conveyed to them in messages from the tarot cards, crystal ball,
and psychometry—simply by touching your hands, an article
of clothing, or whatnot!"

"Watch the fat lady eat!" the freak-show barker vied for the
carnival-goers' attention. "See her pack away pound after
pound of food. Right before your eyes!"

"You know the worth of readings from the famous Ravachek
seers! We've traveled this country east to west, north to south,
for three generations. You've read newspaper copy about the
famous Ravachek women: Rava, Zita, and now another gifted
seer in a long line of family psychics—Mademoiselle Lolita!
Individual readings for only two bits, one quarter of a dollar!
Satisfaction guaranteed—or your money cheerfully refunded."

Lolly almost laughed out loud over that promise.

She hadn't been very old when they'd been at a weekend
engagement, heaven knew where, and someone hadn't appreciated Aunt Zita's reading and had demanded his money back.

It had not been *cheerfully* refunded—such money never had
been, and as far as Lolly figured, never would be. Granted, the
man had walked away with the coin returned to the pocket of
his serge trousers. But he was unaware that Aunt Zita, in the
dark of the night, had seen fit to counter what had been a cold-
ly cheerful smile with the most potent of gypsy curses.

They never heard the fate of the man. For they moved on at
break of day, after all. But Lolly had no doubt that if he thought
that Aunt Zita had given him a harsh reading, one that he found
not to his liking, it was probably nothing compared to the curse-
filled future that his rancor had won for him....

"See pictures of the snake man! Half snake and half man.
Spoon-feed Lulabelle the fat lady! Hold Mr. Tiny on your
very own lap!" the freak-show barker cried.

Lolly recognized in his tone a timbre of desperation that signaled that carnival-goers were lining up in front of the ticket booth manned by Lolly's fourteen-year-old brother, Boris, faster than they were queuing up to purchase tickets to gawk at the obese Lulabelle and her tiny companion.

"Step right up, folks. Find out what Lolita can tell you about your future!"

Lolly Ravachek hastily snuffed out the cheroot she'd swiped from Anton, exhaled a stream of acrid smoke, and finished shuffling the tarot cards. The jewels on her fingers—stolen—twinkled and flashed in the dim light.

Lolly stared into the crystal ball, as she had done all day, until her eyes felt gritty and her head ached from the effort. Concerning her own future, it remained infuriatingly murky and indistinct. Her future, surprisingly, was hidden from her at present.

Had Anton—or Zita—cursed her? Lolly was helpless not to idly wonder, for the crystal ball *had* predicted vicious family squabbling months back when things had been pleasant. Back then Lolly had hoped the ball was wrong, even as, with a sinking feeling, she realized it was right. Time—and gypsy temperament—had borne out the crystal ball's validity. In recent months past, Anton and his sister, Zita, had argued and bickered as never before. Resentments ran high in Lolly. At times, she considered sneaking a peek into the ancient books in Grandma Rava's trunk and leveling a curse at Anton and Zita herself, but she couldn't quite bring herself to do it.

They were, after all, her family, and she felt loyalty to them.

That loyalty, however, had been shaken when one night, in the midst of the dark still broken only by nocturnal circus noises from restless animals—which kept few circus people awake—Lolly had been awakened by Anton and Zita's raspy whispers as they hurled invectives at one another.

Anton had called Zita a most unflattering name.

In response, Zita had squalled like the she-cat she was.

"Don't come up against me, Anton Ravachek, for you shall be the loser!" Zita had taunted. "You know that my powers are much more tremendous than your own weak strengths. Have you so easily forgotten what happened before? Think, Anton! Do you want to risk *that* again?. . ."

There had been a horrid silence.

It had been broken a minute later by the muted, coughing sound of Anton choking on sobs that he tried to keep muffled.

"I rid the family of your beloved wife when she began to get in the family's way. . . . I can do it again . . . and I will . . . so if you are wise, my stupid little brother, you will not cross me again."

"You took my Katrina from me—I beg of you, do not destroy Lolly!"

"I probably shan't have to!" Zita had sneered. "As taken with her powers as she is, she'll likely become so possessed of herself that she'll find her own bad end—and I shan't have to go to the trouble and bother of casting a spell!. . ."

"Don't! In the name of all the gods that we hold sacred—don't!"

"We shall see," Zita had said, her tone mysterious. "We shall see. Lolly has a fate . . . yes . . . but she holds that fate in her own hands. . . . What she chooses in the future will seal her fate. . . ."

The next day, Lolly had tried to attend to daily life as if she hadn't overheard the fight, but whenever she sensed Zita's eyes upon her, she was helpless not to stare back, her own gaze as studying as her aunt's as the older woman seemed to take Lolly's measure and find her wanting.

After that, Anton had seemed more subdued, more submissive, when it came to Zita. Grandma Rava had started to fail. And Boris, who knew that someday the Ravachek family business would be his, had begun to assist his father more and more.

Lolly felt bereft, even as the gay hurdy-gurdy ground out day after day, week after week. She was bitterly alone, even when crowds of people were pressed up against her in the steamy summer sunshine.

Grandma Rava was the only bright spot in Lolly's world, and it was a bright spot that seemed to fade more with each passing day. They knew, without consulting the tools of their trade, that Grandma Rava would soon die.

Rava Ravachek knew it, too. She'd spent a lot more time alone, ordering that others give her privacy, as she consulted her crystal ball and tarot cards. She'd leafed through the ancient books with cracked leather bindings and faint gold embossing that were faithfully packed along with the family, never out of Grandma Rava's possession—just as they'd never left the ownership of the one who'd bequeathed the items to the strangely talented Rava.

The family had known that before she drew her last breath, Rava Ravachek would pass the precious family heirlooms on to a blood relative, pray incantations over that chosen individual, and transfer her own vast powers to an heir and protégé.

There had been an air of tension that pervaded the entire family and even seemed to flow out to other members of the circus troupe, who sensed that something was afoot within the Ravachek encampment and, although they asked no questions, regarded the various members of the family with curious eyes.

Who would be the Chosen to follow Rava in leadership of the fortune-telling family?

Anton?

Zita?

Lolita?

Or Boris?...

The days of waiting for the answer to be given had come a fortnight earlier.

Grandma Rava had called Lolly in to have a private audience with her, while the rest of the family was banished from their presence—and they had all known what it meant.

Anton had looked both fearful and crestfallen.

Zita had been livid.

Boris had been indifferent. He'd had other things on his mind that held greater precedence, and he'd actually been grateful to be ordered away from the family tent for a while so he could be about more leisurely business.

"It's in the blood, Lolly," Grandma Rava had quietly explained, droning on and on as she told stories of the family, going through the lineage with which Lolly was already somewhat familiar.

"The day will come when you too will pass this ball on to another who is chosen. When it is time—the ball itself will reveal to you to whom it is to go...."

"I see...."

"It takes a strong human spirit to bear the woes of all those whose lives and futures are laid bare for us to see so clearly. But the Chosen One can withstand ... or would not have been among those selected. It is an honor, child, and for that, give thanks to your ancestors, who've found you worthy and willing. Draw near, child," Rava had commanded.

Touching Lolly's forehead, her eyes, her lips, her ears, her heart, she had mumbled ancient incantations in a solemn rite. Then she had sprinkled an odd-smelling dust over Lolly, made strange gestures over the crystal ball before ceremoniously picking it up in her gnarled, bony, age-spotted hands, extending it toward Lolly, who reached for it with a smooth, strong, youthful grip.

"The ball is now yours. . . ," Madame Rava had said.

"Thank you, Grandma."

" . . . And the books." The old woman had given an imperceptible nod toward the trunk. "And the wisdom within them."

"I'll cherish and use them."

"And the powers that were once upon a time passed to me—I now pass to you, Lolly Ravachek. . . . Bow your head. . . . Close your eyes. . . ."

Lolly had done as she was told.

"Great powers have been entrusted to you. Guard the heirlooms—and your abilities—with your life. Give them your life! In return, they will guide you well if you respect and revere the powers that possess you. Then someday when you are old, when you are tired . . . someday . . . someday. . . ."

Lolly had nodded, feeling suddenly strong, vibrant, and wise. She'd understood what her grandmother had been too weak to speak. One day she, Lolly Ravachek, would pass down the family beliefs and heirlooms to another in their lineage.

When the others had been allowed entrance into the Ravachek domicile, few words were spoken, but the air was heavy with knowledge, and Lolly was aware of the variety of glances that were cast in her direction when other family members thought she was not looking.

Lolly had been helpless not to feel magnified in her new position of power within the family. She hadn't reckoned on the marked changes that had transpired. Word had obviously traveled quickly through the circus grapevine. Even the few friends she'd known had seemed more respectful—and less playful—as if somehow they had come to fear her rather than view her as a fun-loving, easygoing friend.

Now Lolly had two crystal balls, the one she'd had since she was a child—a gift from Grandma Rava—and the family heirloom.

Previously Lolly and others had been forbidden to stare into the family heirloom that was Rava's property, held in trust even as she used it as her own. When it had suddenly been Lolly's right to do so, she wasn't wholly comfortable— for the family heirloom seemed to possess powers vastly different from the ball that Lolly had used to envision futures of paying customers since her childhood.

Grandma Rava had confidence that Lolly would master the heirloom artifacts. And indeed Lolly noticed that after she'd received the strange blessing from her grandmother, her own powers of perception increased. But it was as if . . . almost like . . . Grandma Rava's crystal ball was *angry* . . . and had become uncooperative!

"What do you see?" Aunt Zita archly inquired of Lolly when she sat in stolid silence, unmoving, and stared trance-like into the crystal ball that rested on an ornate, antique brass base.

"It's not for you to ask, Zita Ravachek! Nor for Lolly to tell! Mind your mouth!" Madame Rava snapped.

"Mama!" Zita protested.

"You know better . . .," Rava sighed.

"Keep it to yourself!" Zita cast the muttered comment in Lolly's direction, contenting herself that she'd at least had the last word.

"I will . . .," Lolly casually murmured in return.

Then she turned away from the ball and closed and rubbed her weary eyes.

What, oh what, did the strange, chaotic, conflicting images mean?

It was so, so confusing.

It was as if the ball were filled with dark and swirling storm clouds. Then there was a split in the darkness, as if a thunderous sky had been rent, and suddenly there were majestic rays, like the brightest of sunlight streaming from the heavens, and they intercepted to form a golden cross of light that was cameoed against a breathtakingly beautiful, paradise-like scene.

But it only lasted a moment—such a brief time—before the black clouds swept back in, heavier, thicker, impenetrable, and there was only utter blackness and a sensation that left Lolly feeling wholly and totally lost. . . .

Grandma Rava had said that the powers were a gift and an honor, but Lolly had her moments when she wasn't so sure. She wasn't so sure it was an honor . . . but she knew only too well that hers was a hurtful burden that must be borne. . . .

chapter
3

Williams, Minnesota

"STILL AN EARLY riser, are you, Lem Gartner?" Lizzie cheerfully called over her shoulder, her voice carrying into the massive hotel lobby when she recognized Lemont's footsteps on the stairwell. A moment later he was beside her, spry and grinning.

"That I am!"

"As am I," Lizzie said.

"Might you have a few moments to take a break, Miss Lizzie, especially iffen I were to help you rustle together the morning vittles?"

It seemed an odd request. Lizzie consulted her watch brooch.

"Mayhap a few moments. You've something special in mind?"

Lemont nodded. "We didn't have the privacy last evening, and by end of day, I'm afraid I was too tired in my body to attend to what was in my heart. And bless you, Lizzie, for not even expecting it of me. . . ."

"Oh. Well . . . yes. . . ." She was aware of to what he referred.

"Didn't even take time to unpack last night, 'ceptin' for my nightshirt. But it was my first order of the day for this morn."

"You have Thad's things unpacked?"

Lem nodded and gave her arm a mute pat.

29

"I can afford a few moments. For this the customers can just wait 'n be patient!"

"I doubt that any of them would begrudge you the moments to attend to such a matter. Especially not when they're able to wait over a cup of your fresh coffee."

"Smells good, don't it? We'll pause for a cup after we . . . after we . . . attend to . . ."

Suddenly Lizzie was too choked up to speak, and Lemont found a mealy lump stuck in his own throat. He settled for nodding as he followed Lizzie back up the stairwell and down the hall to his quarters.

"There's his things. On the bed," Lemont said when Lizzie opened up the door from the dim hallway and morning light revealed the items arranged on the crisply remade bed.

Overcome, Lizzie crossed the room in quick steps, then fell to her knees beside the bed, as if to enfold a beloved child.

Her work-hardened hands, showing signs of age, tenderly closed around a worn copy of the Good Book.

" . . . Thad's Bible . . .," she whispered.

Lem laid an understanding hand on her shoulder, then cleared his throat. "As his mama, Miss Lizzie, you can draw real comfort from just how well-worn that Bible is from Thad's use."

Lizzie regarded the leather-bound volume. She was helpless not to smile through gathering tears when her fingertips fanned open the book and her touch caressed the pages that had grown soft and velvety beneath years of Thad's flipping through its pages.

"Oh . . . here's a smear o' blackberry jam!" Lizzie softly cried, laughing. "I remember the mornin' that happened! I had given the Good Book to Thad for Christmas, and whilst on Christmas vacation afore the new school year started, he dropped a drip o' sticky ol' jam on it. He was so devastated that I didn't even bother to growl at him. Just cleaned it up as best I could. Managed to remove the stickies—but the stain stayed on."

"Did he learn his lesson?" Lemont asked.

Lizzie gave her head a slow, rueful shake. "My Thad? Of course not! 'Twas years and many stains later, I'm afraid, before he matured enough to make sure his hands were clean."

"Reckon he was always feedin' his body along with his spirit, aye?" Lem pointed out.

"Reckon so!" Lizzie judged. "He did like to bury his nose in a book, that boy."

"Don't you expect that the Lord would have a taste for your blackberry jam himself, Miss Lizzie?"

"I'd be honored to serve it to him. . . ."

"In my view, I'm helpless not to figure that the Lord would cotton more to a Bible with some jam smears than he'd have cottoned to a Bible with pristine pages—'n dust on the cover."

"I'd think so, too. Hope so. . . ."

"There are other gewgaws. A few trinkets in the drawstring pouch, too."

One by one, Lizzie examined the articles as she and the elderly neighbor reflected on days gone by and a young life once so vibrantly lived.

"Oh! Here's his prize shootin' marble!" Lizzie cried. "And his first pocket knife. The ivory toothpick my mama gave him."

"Don't forget the yo-yo!" Lemont said. "Wasn't a young'un in the neighborhood who could work that contraption like your Thad."

"And his Jew's harp. Heavens but he liked to have drove us crazy playin' that thing. As many times as I ragged at him to go outside with that fool harp, now I'd invite folks into the parlor to hear him play, iffen only he were here to do so."

As Lemont and Lizzie laughed, then shed tears before chuckling all over again as they browsed in the museum of memories that Lemont had brought with him, the strain within the room became almost overwhelming.

Suddenly they were both racked with tears and clung to each other, sobbing their shared grief.

"I miss him so, Lem! Sometimes I can hardly stand it! Not knowin' what became of him or where his body's final restin' place even is likes to almost drive me to distraction at times."

"I know, Miss Lizzie. Not knowin' is a lot worse than knowin' and bein' able to face it with factual finality."

"I know it ain't to be, and it ain't right to even feel this way, to be sometimes so questioning. But oh, if only there was someone who could somehow tell me exactly what happened to my boy and clarify his fate, it'd ease my burden as a grievin' ma."

"One day, Miss Lizzie, we'll all know, when we see the Lord face-to-face."

" . . . Until then I reckon I'll be condemned to . . . wonderin'. . . ."

Redwing, Minnesota

Lolly Ravachek stood on the bluff overlooking the Mississippi River, staring across, as if sightless, at the Wisconsin shoreline so near yet so far away.

Tears unceasingly streamed down her cheeks, making her wonder if they would gather to such a degree that the water level would rise.

"Are you coming or not?" Zita snapped.

Lolly couldn't even speak. She was too miserable for words. She settled for a shrug.

The gesture infuriated her aunt, who'd grown more difficult by the day and had grown even more shrewish with Grandma Rava's passing the evening before — having to attend to all the necessary requirements, forms, and red tape that a migrant death had caused.

"Oh . . . grow up, you silly child!" Zita hissed. "Who are the tears for? Rava? Or Lolly? All the sobs in the world won't bring her back. All you'll do is trouble her spirit with your carrying on! Selfish, that's what you are: *selfish!* Dying's the expected end result of living, so face it! We've got enough troubles in this without you making your miseries a problem to us."

Lolly clenched her fists, refusing to turn around to look at the older, hated woman.

" . . . Leave . . . me . . . alone! . . .," she whispered from between gritted teeth.

Although her words were faint, Zita overheard.

Her reaction was a wail that duplicated the bray of a jackass as indignation escalated to raw rage.

"Maybe we just will! 'Tis no treat to have your company, Miss! Stay here! See if we care! I shan't waste my breath to say good-bye but would consider it an effort well invested to utter good riddance!"

"Then leave . . .," Lolly muttered, her voice faint but hard.

A wave of anguish knifed through her at the thought of never seeing Anton or Boris Ravachek again, but the anguish was driven away by anger as fiery as her aunt's. Suddenly she whirled, as if possessed by a force other than herself.

Her eyes narrowed and her tawny complexion drained limpid except for livid splashes of red at her cheeks.

"I should die a happy woman if I never saw hide nor hair of

you again . . . you witch! That's what you are, Zita Ravachek, a nasty old hag, a *witch!*"

"You, my dear, are no better. In fact," Zita said, her face and eyes smug, "you're not even as good. 'Twas *I* who should have inherited Mama Rava's heirlooms!"

"They were meant for me—the Chosen!" Lolly flared.

Zita gave a scornful, braying laugh. "Beware, Lolly . . . *beware!* Even without Mama Rava's powers transferred to me and added to my own, I shall call forth demons and spirits to bedevil you for all of your days. They'll be the end of you— and you shall help them in their destruction of you. Then I shall dance on your grave!"

The specter of not only losing Grandma Rava, who had been buried in a pauper's plot in a cemetery overlooking the Mississippi, but also being robbed of her heritage, and losing the only items that Lolly had to link her to her beloved grandmother, spurred her into action.

Without a word, she turned on her heel and then ran, fast and in a way most unladylike, toward the Ravachek tent. Her ribs stabbed with the effort of each breath, but she knew that she could outdistance the older Zita, pluck up her belongings, cram them into a satchel, and dash away to hide where the nasty witch couldn't find her.

Ten minutes later, pressed into a thicket of brush that created a labyrinth, Lolly peered through the dappling leaves, holding her breath when her searching aunt drew near. Lolly prayed, to the powers that protected her, not to be detected.

Finally Lolly watched Zita move away, not even looking back, as she apparently gave up on her for the time being, but Lolly sensed that she would be back, so she beseeched the myriad spirits to protect her with an impenetrable cover that would prevent her wicked relative from discovering her whereabouts.

It was a long time after the woman had disappeared from sight when Lolly winced, twisted, and pried herself out of the tangle of briars and bushes, extracting her earthly possessions behind her.

Suddenly she felt woefully alone.

She wanted desperately to return to Grandma Rava's graveside one last time, but she wiped tears, then forced herself to turn away from the sentimental thought, aware that her aunt might expect her to return to the paltry plot and could be waiting even now to capture her—and the family heirlooms that were now hers.

The townspeople of Redwing had been receptive enough when the carnival was in town, but after the bands of gypsies and carnival workers moved on—Lolly wondered what lie Zita must have told the family about her running away—the residents of the small river city looked upon her with distaste and distrust. More than a few ordered her, in harsh voices, to hie on out of town before she was run out on a rail! Not that she really minded, for she was in a frenzied rush to put as much distance between herself and her aunt as was humanly possible.

"She's the fortune-teller from the circus!" she overheard herself identified several times.

And then vicious, judgmental indictments were leveled against her.

"Witch! We'll not suffer a witch to live among us!"

"Leave whilst you still have life within ye!"

Miserable, Lolly began trudging out of town, unsure of where she was going. Lolly was burning with rejection and resentment. She fairly itched to stop, dig through her valise, locate Grandma Rava's ancient books of occult wisdom, and place a curse on the entire region.

But she realized that first she must put distance between

herself and the townspeople—as well as her own lineage. It was safer that way.

The nerve of them, she raged inwardly—smarting with hurt and anger. Those do-gooders had railed in her face over what an evil person she was, when they didn't even really *know* her. Why, she knew full well that most of them were no better than she—and some of them, she could personally testify, were undoubtedly a lot, lot worse!

Especially when she compared the stable, wholesome normalcy of their upbringing with the itinerant, pillar-to-post, circus-freak aspects of her own upraising that had been established from the moment of her conception, with a circus trunk serving as her crib when she was born into this world.

By the time dusk began to fall, Lolly sought a place to lay her head for the night. Fortunately, the sky was clear, and she was reassured that she wouldn't be caught out in the open in a deluge.

Near a slow-moving brook, Lolly located a private glade shielded from the easy detection of those who passed by, and she placed her valise on the ground, unfurled the one thin blanket she'd thought to yank along with her, and seated herself to rest, wishing that she had something with which to appease her hunger.

She was worrying about what the morrow would bring, when she laughed out loud, then with focused intent withdrew the carefully wrapped crystal ball from within the shelter of the valise.

She didn't know what to do. But she didn't have to know. Her crystal ball would provide all the answers she would ever need in life. She needn't trust her own wits—when she had faith in the crystal ball's magical revelations.

Visions in the ball were wondrous!

Fame!

Fortune!

Fun!

That night Lolly fell asleep feeling at peace for the first time in all of her seventeen years.

Come the dawn, she would neaten up a bit, enter the town that noises testified was just over the next hill or two, and she would learn if the beguiling fate that was to be hers awaited her there.

And if not, she'd move on, guided by ancient wisdom, until she found the spot in life established for her by all the unseen powers that had chosen her as their own.

Shantytown
The Mississippi River

River traffic was light. An ethereal, hazy mist hung over the broad river, which was languid toward the banks but fast-moving midchannel, its rippling current dimpling the water's surface.

The young man—who appeared to be in his early twenties—sat on a large boulder on the bluff overlooking the Mississippi. His deeply tanned face was protected from the sun's searing kiss, which had darkened his skin to a burnished copper, by a dappling of leaves overhead.

There was something that drew him to the mighty river to rest and reflect. It was quietly peaceful there, enveloping him in nature's tranquillity yet at the same time haunting him, seemingly day and night. It was as if the water that shielded treasures and potential tragedies beneath its depths somehow contained the secret of who he was, where he was from, and how he'd ended up in a poor river shantytown in an area that he sensed had not been home to him—even though at present it was the only existence he knew or remembered.

The young man had heard black folks in the shantytown, who'd been born on the riverbanks and lived there all of their lives, refer to the mighty Mississippi as if it were literally part of the family, one capable of performing various roles.

In one wide tributary was found the capacity to behave like a whimsically playful sibling, generous grandfather, doting mother, and stern, taskmaster father.

Folks spoke of the Mississippi as if it were a living, breathing entity with personality traits they knew as well as the familiar foibles of the closest of kin, with strengths to cherish and flaws to overlook and learn to live with.

At times even murderous, the Mississippi captured the living within its depths—but eventually it would cooperatively give up its dead to their mourners.

The young man with no name—at least none that he could recall, save the moniker given him by the black folks who'd taken him in—stared down at the wide river as if waiting for it to finally give up what he sensed were dark secrets, like bloated, putrefying corpses ghoulishly bobbing to the surface, startling those who confronted them and were called upon to deal with macabre reality.

Think! the man mentally ordered himself.

He tried—oh, how hard he tried!. . .

It seemed as if the very veins at his neck and temples bulged and throbbed with the force of his inner effort, to the point where he felt light-headed from the strain. He felt a sudden wave of dizzy exhaustion, even though it was but the break of day and he'd again slept dreamlessly the evening past. The man drew a ragged breath and dropped his face into his hands, rubbing at his eyelids, pushing and massaging downward on his handsomely boned cheeks, trying to alleviate the grinding ache that seemed to radiate outward from a fresh scar, pink with healing, that slashed across his left temple.

A moment later, as one in a trance, he stared down at the river, waiting . . . waiting . . . for he knew not what. . . .

The River Queen

Nanette was awake come the dawn, and when she looked outside her cabin porthole, she felt a sudden shadow of sadness wash over her. Unless she was totally mistaken, they were not far from the spot where her brother, Nicholas, and Thad Childers had fought and her brother had shot Thad, causing him to fall overboard and drown.

She was helpless not to wonder how her life might be different if Thad had only lived and they'd been able to remain together and become joined in the Lord. . . .

When Nanette's heart was heavy, she was drawn, as if by rote, to her reticule. From it she extracted a pleasantly thick envelope bearing a Williams, Minnesota, postmark and freed the sheets so she could reread Lizzie Mathews' letter—again.

Dear Lizzie, Nanette thought.

There was comfort in being a correspondent with her late beau's mother. Nanette realized that it gave Lizzie peace to be in touch with her, too.

As soon as she'd solidified her travel plans, she'd written her itinerary to Lizzie, promising to write and asking Lizzie and the community church to remember her in prayers and to drop her a note whenever time allowed.

What she hadn't told Lizzie was that more and stronger, with each passing day, was a call to her heart to travel from the mouth of the Mississippi all the way up past its headwaters in northern Minnesota so that she could personally make the acquaintance of the family whose love and values had formed the man with whom she'd briefly—and passionately—been in love.

It was something that she had to do.

And now, with the generous gift harvested from the money tree, she knew that she could afford to travel a bit farther on her own, arrive at the Grant Hotel in Williams, register to stay, and either she'd be as welcomed as she hoped or she'd at least be received with the hospitality extended to any paying guest.

Nanette, an orphan who'd not long known a mother's loving arms and had too frequently borne a father's cruel slaps and cuffs, ached to reach out to and touch the woman who'd carried Thad beneath her heart and held him in her arms until he was old enough that she could only stand back and entrust him to the Lord when he set out to explore the tempting world that had waited to ensnare him—as it had Nanette.

In his desperation to free her, Thad had surely found his own liberation from the dark forces that had dragged him down to death, which for him was but a passing from tribulation into triumph. . . .

Shantytown

"Yo! Rib! Ya'll here? . . ."

From a short distance away, a husky, dusky, southern-inflected voice drifted through the hazy and humid morning air to the young man on the bluff overlooking the river.

"Over here . . . Amos . . .," he called back, gesturing.

The words came from his mouth as if they were slowly and with some difficulty dislodged and extracted from his mind.

The young man sensed—and it was a torment to him—that his head was like a dusty, cobwebby alcove of events and information, a veritable museum of memories if only he could locate the secret passageway that would allow him entrance to explore the recorded intellectual artifacts collected during a lifetime that he could no longer remember.

A moment later a strongly muscled, stoutly built, bibbed overalls–clad black youth bounded toward Rib, his bare feet slapping the damp, cool ground, a happy grin splitting his features.

"What y'all doin', Rib?"

" . . . Waitin' . . . for . . . Just waitin'. . . ."

Amos grinned.

"Waitin' for de *Rib' Queen*, ain't ya?"

Rib didn't answer.

Amos craned around and upward to consult the sun's position, then glanced downriver.

"She be comin' 'round de bend purt' directly," Amos said. "Be a-hearin' 'er bellow afore that. . . ." No sooner had the black man made the prediction than from just downriver and around the bend came the faint, froggy moan of the paddle wheeler's horn, muted by the humid air and the trees that blocked their view of the river beyond the bend.

Rib seemed to perk up at the sound, growing alert, tensed, like a good bird dog on point.

Amos, observing, gave a warm chuckle and joyfully cuffed Rib's arm, as if to share in a private joke, although it was one the Shantytown native didn't fully understand.

"Yo' shore is 'tached to dat ol' boat, ain't ya?"

Rib shrugged.

He didn't know what to say.

Maybe he was. He had to be—if Amos said it was so.

"Stands to reason, Ah reckons," Amos mused. "After all, Rib, dat's de boat dat'd just passed by, goin' south, when we fetched yo' out o' de water. Yo' din't know who yo' was—we din't know who yo' be—and Sis, she end up callin' yo'

'Rib'er Boy', 'n de name stuck. Been shortened down to 'Rib' over de passin' o' time."

Rib nodded. That he'd been told.

"It don' make us no nevermind what we all calls yo'. We don' know who yo' are—but den, neither do yo'!"

Rib shrugged again. He did know one thing—and that was that he didn't know who he was. And it seemed that when he tried so hard to remember, his head filled to throbbing with a strange pain from the effort. It soon became easier to stop even trying to recall than suffer the frustrating, painfully grinding sensation and resulting headaches. Easier to just give it no thought at all.

"Mayhap one o' dese days, yo'll see de *Rib' Queen,* and the sight o' dat ol' boat will bring yo' thoughts jus' flooding back like de Mississippi int' her flood plains come spring! Memories be just *ever'where* then! Yo'll know who yo' be—'n den yo' kin tell us!"

Amos spoke with more conviction and optimism than he really felt. It had been months and months since he and his brother, Luke, had been night-fishing along the Mississippi River and almost got run over by the *River Queen.* They'd heard a gunshot, a loud splash, paddled for all they were worth to get away, and then no sooner had they turned their pirogue for shore and home than Luke's oar had struck something, causing Amos' younger brother to squawk in bone-wilting alarm.

Amos had held the lantern aloft, adjusted the wick—burning up precious coal oil—for a better look, and Luke, who was afraid of haunts and ghosts, almost turned inside out to realize that they'd just poled their pirogue into a corpse!

"Let's fish 'im out," Amos had said. "He deserves a decent burial at least!"

"Ah ain't touchin' him!" Luke had squalled, backing up until he almost fell off the end of the pirogue and into the river with the drowned man.

"Den get out o' my way. Ah'll tend to it mahself!"

Luke had whimpered and gibbered in fright—and was cajoled into at least holding the lantern only when Amos threatened to cuff him a good one.

Luke, with bated breath, had watched as Amos gingerly leaned out and snagged at the drowned gent's fancy clothing with the sturdy end of a short cane fishing pole.

As if he were teasing a scab loose, he'd edged the bobbing corpse toward the boat.

"Row, Luke, 'n we kin tow him to shore wit' me hangin' on to him. Unless yo' goin' to help lug de gent int' the pirogue, 'n then Ah'll row, too. . . ."

Luke had quickly moved into place and allowed that he'd sooner row all by himself than share a pirogue with a dead white man.

"Be slow 'n steady 'bout it," Amos had cautioned.

"Cain't get to sho' fast 'nuff to suit *me!*" Luke had yelped, and he began to paddle zealously.

Amos had struggled to hang on to the gentleman's vest. The silky, wet fabric eventually gave way with a damp *rriiiiii-iip!* and in his desperation not to lose the river's victim—and without bothering to consult Luke—Amos, gasping for breath and straining for leverage, hauled the drowning victim into the pirogue.

With a thud, he had landed in the bottom of the craft in a sodden heap. The pirogue shifted, and Luke, caught without warning, shrieked and leaped into the water—oar, coal oil lantern, and all.

"Yo' li'l fool!" Amos had cried out when the cold water

caused the hot lantern globe to shatter and then the night was inky black.

"Where yo' be at, Amos?" Luke had burbled as he tried to swim without releasing any of the family's possessions.

"Close to shore! Swim dere yo'self! Bet' yet, swim on over here, Ah'll fetch de lantern, 'n yo' can hang on to de boat while Ah rows us all to shore. . . ."

Minutes later the pirogue had bumped into the bank of the Mississippi. Luke clambered ashore and held the pirogue steady as Amos wrestled the drowned man up onto his shoulder. He sloshed through the shallow, slick mud where water met soil, tripped, lost his balance, and fell with a thud, landing on the chest of the man he'd been carrying.

"Iffen he wasn't dead," Luke had said, "yo'd have kilt him for sure, landin' on him like dat! Yo' best be hopin' someone don' come along—'n think yo' done him in, boy!"

"Hush yo' mouth!" Amos had ordered.

In remembering and retelling the tale to Rib yet one more time, now, months later, Amos gave a rich, amused chuckle.

"Ah was scared, sho' nuff, dat a lynch party o' dem KKK men in dey sheets might happen 'pon us. Luke and me, we's squintin' in de dark at each other, tryin' ter fig' out what t' do. Then all o' de sudden dere's dis squishy runnin' sound. Ah turns 'round fast-like. Hooked m' foot in dat raggedy vest o' yo's, 'bout broke m' toe on yo' ribs, 'n water run like blood from yo' nose!

"Luke, he's yowlin' 'bout what happens 'ter folks dat's dis-'spectful t' de daid 'n riles up dem ghosts 'n haints. Well, Rib, 'bout dat time, yo' lets out wit' this gurgly cough. Lawsy mercy, but it be *turrible!*

"Plumb scared Luke 'n me so's we din't know what ter do! We's bot' tryin' to get 'way from yo', trips int' each oth', 'n boths of us falls int' de water—*ker-plop!* Yo' was gaggin' 'n coughin', 'n Luke 'n me stood dere in de rib' 'fraid to let go o' each other. After while, yo' began moanin', 'n Ah realize' yo' wasn' no ghost or haint—not drowned, neither—jus' hurt bad!. . . Now ain't dat a funny story? But sho' as Ah be settin' here 'side yo', dat's what done happened!"

Amos grinned.

Rib shrugged.

"Dere she comes!" Amos cried out when the *River Queen* fully rounded the bend and grandly steamed up the Mississippi toward their vantage point. "Ain' she a sight? Ah'd sho' like to climb 'board dat steamer someday 'n travel wit' such fine 'commodations! Heavens! Sho' do wisht yo' could 'member what it be like so's yo' could tell me a fine story all 'bout it!. . ."

Rib listened, then shrugged.

Amos sighed. "Don' guess yo' members none o' dat yet. Mayhap nev' will."

". . . No . . .," Rib said, and his hesitant tone revealed a tinge of uncertainty over even the basic meaning of the very word he used.

Exuberant as he always got over seeing the stately steamship, Amos had leaped to his feet, jumping up and down and waving. Usually his exertions went unnoticed. But this time, the pilot of the paddle wheeler must've seen him, for a deep, throaty but merry toot had been his answering call.

This was followed by another sound. "C'mon, Rib! Don' yo' hear de break'fus bell? Mama's got the grits 'n fried side meat ready! Le's go! Ah'm hungry! De way Mama be singin' dis morn'n, Ah knows she's gots a 'specially fine meal!"

Amos, plowing up the path toward the shanty, added his own exuberant strains to his mama's rendition of "Amazing

Grace," which was punctuated by clangs of the pump as she drew water from the cistern.

"Hurry'p!" Amos encouraged.

Rib shrugged. Then nodded.

Amazing.

Grace.

Sweet.

What next?

THINK!

chapter

4

Redwing, Minnesota

FOOTWEARY AND FAMISHED, shortly after the dawning of a new day, Lolly Ravachek plodded into the nondescript upriver town, so like the other small hamlets that dotted the banks along the Mississippi that Lolly hadn't even bothered to inquire as to its name.

Aware of her dwindling funds but casting her fate to the wind, she approached a hotel with an adjoining dining room, laid down her money, and got a room to let.

The first day, she did nothing but rest and eat her fill.

The second day, she explored the town.

The response was not what she expected—and was counter to the wondrous future the crystal ball had promised.

"Begone with you! I'll not tolerate a thieving gypsy in our midst! I'd druther trust a yellar dog!"

"We'll not endure your type in this God-fearing town!" an old woman shrilly warbled and shook a heavy black book after Lolly. "Perhaps they'll allow the likes of you and put up with your crafts and incantations in those big-city Babylons! We in this village won't suffer your abominable presence!"

Lolly had grown up in a family that knew what it was not to be wanted, and when they sensed that they'd worn out their welcome—or depleted a community's available funds—they resolutely moved on. And not heavy with resignation but usually filled with optimism and good cheer in belief of the fortune to be found around the next bend in the road.

Carefully packing her crystal ball after consulting it and seeing a train revealed in its misty center, Lolly was aware that she was to invest what remained of her funds to purchase a ticket to more quickly take her where she was destined to go.

She was limping by the time she let herself into the depot.

The agent looked up with an inquiring expression.

"Help you?"

" . . . Yes. I'd like a ticket to . . . to . . . Babylon," she said, straining to remember the old woman's shrill suggestion. She glared when the ticket agent swallowed a muffled laugh.

"Ain't no Babylon in these parts, miss," he informed. "Reckon the closest thing to it is either Minneapolis or St. Paul. . . ."

"How much to get there?" Lolly asked.

He named a fee.

The fact that it was *exactly* the amount in her purse, right down to the very penny, seemed a lucky omen to Lolly.

"Gimme a ticket!" Lolly commanded, emptying her thread-bare reticule of coins so that it contained only a handkerchief, a comb, a hairbrush, a scrying mirror, and the deck of tarot cards with which she knew she could earn her way in the world.

"Here's your ticket," the counter agent said after he filled in the appropriate lines. He adjusted his green eyeshade as he separated the tickets and offered Lolly her copy.

"Good luck to you, miss!"

Lolly impetuously tossed her head back, causing her thick, wavy hair to cascade around her shoulders.

"I don't need luck anymore, mister—there's fame and fortune ahead of me. All I've got to do is see to it that I'm in the right place at the right time—and the world will be mine!"

Shantytown

Rib followed Amos toward the Jackson family dwelling, a shanty set back from the river a few hundred feet. It was a pitiful structure but no better and no worse than the same type of dwellings that tumbled down around it, so widow Amelia Jackson and her six children considered themselves no less fortunate than their neighbors. They resided in a close-knit community where everyone believed in serving those who were in need out of their own scanty bounty.

As Rib and Amos trudged nearer the shanty, Rib was totally absorbed in his own thoughts, focusing harder and harder and harder, not stopping even when he felt dizzy and thick-headed almost to the point of becoming sick to his stomach beneath the effort.

"Amazing grace . . . how sweet the sound . . ."

Rib's head fairly ached from trying to remember. There was something so hauntingly familiar—yet it remained so far away, lost within the inky depths of his mind.

Amazing!

The subtle little tune that lingered in his mind to accompany the word ceased, and the word itself filled his mind.

Then came strange phrases, in a multitude of voices and a gabbling cacophony of various tones, accents, and inflections, which were almost scary in their unidentifiable intensity.

"That's plumb amazin'!"

"The most amazin' thing happened to me yesterday!"

Then the melody returned to his mind.

"Amazing grace . . . how sweet the sound . . ."

And words.

"Why, ain't you sweet?!"

"He sure does have a sweet tooth!"

"Let's say table grace. . . ."

Minutes later as the Jackson family enjoyed their hearty morning repast, Rib stared at his untouched plate, seeming lost in an eddying whirlpool of chaotic, half-formed, tormentingly incomplete concepts.

"Rib, there be sumpin' wrong with de grits, chile?" Amelia Jackson—who treated Rib as her own, protecting him as one would a backward but sweet child—inquired. Concern was in her soft brown eyes.

Rib shook his head. He didn't know what to say. There was no way to describe what had been taking place in his mind. No way to convey the collage of words and voices and explain it to the only family he could remember, when he could not understand it himself.

Rib began eating, chewing, chewing, but his mind continued to churn.

"Amazing grace . . . how sweet the sound . . . that . . ."
That!
Another word.
That . . . *WHAT?!*
Rib struggled inwardly to the point where he felt as if he were trembling, almost ready to weep with what was denied him.

"Don't take all o' dem biscuits, Luke! Save one fo' me!" Amos interrupted Rib's mental wranglings.

"Ah done saved a few back in de o'vn. Yo' chillun eat hearty . . . ain't much fancy, but it be fillin'. . . ."
Saved!
A euphoria Rib didn't understand but only felt to the core of his being gripped him. He couldn't remember the word, but he recognized the feeling. Something momentous had happened. He so badly wanted to share it with those around him.

"Amazing grace . . . how sweet the sound . . . that saved . . ."
That was as far as he could speak.

"Praise God, it's a mir'cle!" Amelia cried, dropping her fork as she clapped her work-lined hands together and grinned. "Dat boy finally be 'memberin'!" Amelia cried the announcement.

Then, as if somehow guided, perhaps by maternal instinct, she began to sing—in a beautiful, low, rich voice—the old beloved hymn, which wasn't used as often in their church in the black shantytown as some of the spirituals passed down from their ancestors. ". . . the sound that saved a wretch like me . . .," Amelia sang at the breakfast table as those around her held their forks aloft and stared from Amelia to Rib and back again, aware that they were witnessing something miraculous.

WRETCH!

Another word!

"Thad, you little wretch—get out o' that cookie jar!"

A tear pooled in the corner of Rib's eye.

Amelia's voice died away to a silence that was as moving as her impromptu hymn had been inspirational.

Then another tear formed, and the weight caused the moisture to spill over. A lone tear trailed down Rib's cheek. He stared in mute wonderment at what was seeping into his mind, not with a rush but a slow, steady, beautiful trickle, like a soddening spring rain that would make the timber blossom anew.

"C'mon, Thad . . . let's hie on out to the timber and pick Mama a bouquet of spring flowers for a surprise!"

Who was that pretty and sweet girl?

He didn't know . . . yet.

But he sensed with all his heart that at last he knew who *he* was.

He faced the Jackson family, rapt brown faces surrounding him.

"My . . . my . . . name is . . . *Thad!*. . ." There was a stunned silence, then they cheered and applauded.

"Ain't this grand?" Amelia said.

"Look't what yo' singin' done, Mama!" Luke said.

"Ah be thinkin' it be the words more'n my d'livery,"

Amelia said. Then she was struck by an idea. "Y'all know the song. Let's sing it to Rib—Ah mean *Thad*—again. And dis time, let's lift our voices t' praise the Lawd. Iffen yo'll sing the reg'lar tune, den Ah'll play 'round wit' the harmony...."

HARMONY!

Another word.

So many meanings ...

As the Jacksons sang to him, one tear after another fell from Thad's cheeks, and Amelia Jackson no longer tried to stem them with her fingertip.

I'm Thad, Rib thought, *and my sister is Harmony. We have a ma. We picked her spring flowers in the timber. What's her name? Think ... think ... THINK!...*

Thad tried, but it would not come.

"Don' strain yo'self," Amelia said, recognizing his inner agony. She arose to clear the table, then bent over and gave Thad a motherly hug. As she did, he recognized the scent that she wore. Poor as they were, she managed to scrimp for a little treat for herself and her girls. Thad knew where the bottle was kept. He went to it and held it out to her.

Amelia gave a hearty but confused laugh.

"What yo' doing with that scent water, boy? Surely yo' ain't be wantin' to wear my Lemon Verbena! What you' tryin' ter get at?"

LEMON VERBENA!

More memories.

"*Lemon Verbena is Ma's favorite....*"

"*I got you a little somethin', Lizzie. Figured there wasn't no one else to give you somethin' this Christmas....*"

"*Oh ... Jeremiah!*"

Thad was thunderstruck.

"Ma's name is Lizzie!..." he whispered. "And she likes ... Lemon Verbena...."

chapter
5

LeFave's Landing
The Lake of the Woods, Minnesota

"LOOK! THERE THEY are!" Lizzie cried out. She waved at her son-in-law, Billy LeFave, and Way-Say-Com-a-Gouk, the Chippewa maiden now known as Serenity, who'd become like a daughter to the hotel manager and her husband.

"'Course they are," Brad said when he spotted them seated on split-sapling lawn furniture created by Billy's hand. It was apparent they were taking their ease as they watched for the arrivals from town. Brad consulted his gold pocket watch. "We're arrivin' right when we said we would come back out to fetch Serenity to town after she spent a fortnight visitin' with the tribe."

"It'll be as good to have Serenity under our roof as it is to have Lemont there."

"Y'all keep lettin' rooms for naught," Lemont warned, "'n there won't be any rooms t' let for hire! Now, I've always known you had a strong business sense, Miss Lizzie, but that cain't be smart iffen you're in the hotel biz."

" . . . I know . . .," Lizzie mused.

It was a point that Lizzie and Brad had even quietly discussed a time or two, deciding not to worry about it, for they'd never had so many rooms filled with family that there hadn't been sufficient rooms to rent. But they figured that the day was likely coming, and they'd have to work out other arrangements. They couldn't let down Rose Ames, the owner of the Grant Hotel. And wouldn't.

"Ain't this lovely?" Lizzie exclaimed. "Just look, Lem!"

And he did.

He was silent as he gazed out over what looked like an endless body of water, satiny blue for as far as the eye could see. There was only a hazy line of a slightly different hue at the horizon, where sea gave way to sky.

Pristine white seagulls, their wings shaded with rich gray and sharp black, flapped overhead, their shrill cries echoing over the glassy lake. Here and there a partially submerged boulder was all that broke the lake's mirrorlike surface.

Along the windswept shore, lapped clean by incoming breakers, was a wide beach. The waves created a tonal chart of graduating colors as water content darkened the sand at the water's edge to a damp, deep brown.

The pine trees wafted an almost fruity evergreen scent into the air, and the rustling of birch leaves was like a background melody. Far off to the right the land extended into a long point that sheltered what was the end of a vast bay, and to the far left a desolate pine-thick island erupted from the lake.

Billy's cabin, roomy, well constructed, pleasing to the eye, solidly chinked, and possessed of a masterpiece of a stone fireplace, crested the bluff. A small outbuilding nearby housed tools and implements to shield them from the elements.

A small garden plot was greening nicely, the tender plants maturing, and Billy had constructed a fence to shield it from ravagement by rabbits and white-tailed deer.

"Good to see you!" Billy called out, coming to meet them, Serenity a few paces behind.

Billy gripped Brad's hand, returned Lizzie's hug, then

shook Lemont's hand when Brad introduced them. Serenity, when she was introduced to Lemont, shyly smiled, modestly bowed her head a degree, then extended her grip, seeming to steal the old gent's heart in the process.

Billy showed Lizzie and Brad recent improvements as he gave Lemont a quick tour of his lakeside property.

There was a neatly maintained pathway to a higher rise on the slope where the cabin was constructed. The spot teemed with carefully pruned shrubbery, wildflowers, and a rosebush that was thriving. A whitewashed cross marked the grave, and nearby was a chair Billy had made to rest a bit during his labors or to sink into when he wanted to pray as he visited his beloved wife's final resting spot.

Solemnly the small knot of people strolled toward Harmony's graveside.

"It's a picture of beauty, Will," Lizzie said. "You sure must have a green thumb!"

"Brown, from grappling with the dirt," he said, examining the tips for stains, grinning as he offered them for proof. "That rosebush is doing well enough that given time, anyone who desires can have a start from the bush marking Harmony's grave. . . ."

Lizzie had heard a soft, whimpering snuffle as they'd progressed along. She suspected Serenity was crying, and when she glanced to see the stoic Indian girl furtively wiping tears from her cheeks, she knew. Instinctively Lizzie folded the mourning young girl to her.

"Shh. . . . it's all right . . . cry iffen you want to, darlin', and especially iffen you're needin' to. Tears are a gift from the Lord to help us wash away the pain 'n sadness so's we can heal and know happiness again."

Staring downward, Serenity nodded.

But instead of the words comforting her, they seemed to further break her heart. She clung to Lizzie, whimpering over and over again, "Serenity sorry . . . so, so sorry. Serenity 'pologize. Sorry, sorry."

"You don't have to be ashamed of sheddin' tears, honey," Lizzie said. "You're among people who hurt as you do. . . . Don't apologize for your grief."

Lemont was brushing his own tears as he regarded the lovingly maintained gravesite, and he couldn't quite reconcile himself that the remains of the beautiful, bright, blonde girl who'd been a favorite of everyone in the neighborhood rested beneath the sod at their feet.

"Why . . . ?" he croaked raggedly. *"Why?"*

No one answered his anguished inquiry.

"Why is it that the good die young? Why did Harmony, who had her life ahead of her, have to pass on? Why couldn't it have been someone like me? An old man with his days most behind him?!"

Lizzie put her arm around Lemont's shoulder.

"I've asked that question myself, Lem, and all I know is that the Lord called Harmony home because she'd served her purpose in this life and he needed her. As beautiful as she could sing on earth—we can only imagine how she's singing praises in heaven. . . ."

"I know you're right, Lizzie, but it's hard for me to adjust to this and accept it. It don't make sense! It don't seem fair, even as I know that the Lord's way is best. A bloke can't help but feel like finding fault with it when some evil and wicked feller lives long 'n does well, 'n some salt-of-the-earth type can't get ahead for being kicked in the behind! I wisht someone would tell me why the wicked prosper and so often are long in days when—forgive me for sayin' so—the world might be a heap better place 'thout 'em!"

Silence spiraled.

It seemed as if no one would answer Lem's lament—or could.

Finally Brad spoke up. He clamped his hand to Lem's shoulder in a gesture of sympathetic understanding.

"My thinking is that it's gotta be 'cause the Good Lord's patient 'n long-suffering towards mankind. He's fair as fair as fair can be. So he's pro'bly giving them individuals ever' chance he can to allow 'em to come to him. It says in the Good Book that he wants none to perish—"

"Although some will," Lizzie sadly added.

"By their own choice," Brad pointed out.

"Some folks have a hard time reachin' a decision," Lizzie spoke her sudden thoughts. "Mayhap that's why the Lord lets 'em live on and on. Givin' your life to Christ ain't an easy choice to make, 'n for some it can be nigh on almost impossible. But the Lord, he knows our hearts, so I believe he gives ever'one their fair chance. . . .'n that takes time. Time for us here, 'n time in eternity—well, they're two different concepts, y'know."

"That's true enough. I know the Lord loves good folks who love him," Brad said. "But he also loves the wicked person who's a sinner, 'cause the Lord created that man or woman and knows that person's potential iffen he or she'll let the Lord in their lives. . . ."

"I know that's true enough—but from my human point o' view, 'taint fair!" Lemont maintained.

"That's why someone as fair as the Lord's in charge o' all o' creation," Lizzie said, laughing. "Even though Scripture tells us not to—we seem unable to cease judgin' one another. . . ."

Lemont turned away from Harmony's gravesite.

"Reckon I've felt judged more'n a few times myself," Lem said.

Billy laughed. "I remember onct when Harmony, speakin' to her mama, referred to me as 'a workin' fool,' and when I heard that, I had it construed all wrong. Thought it was an insult, until Ma explained the finer meaning of it."

"I know the feelin', young man," Lemont said and gave Billy's shoulder a friendly touch. "When I was your age, 'n somewhat older, I dearly loved workin' my farm, my horses, plantin' seeds, raisin' up a fine crop, harvestin' it, haulin' it to town to be sold to fill others' needs. My days was from sunup to sundown, 'ceptin' on Sundays, which were the Lord's Day. Used to fry my gizzard when folks'd pass by, maybe hail me over, and say, 'Ain't no rest for the wicked, Lemont.' I always tried to be a good 'n godly fellow. I felt bad every time they seemed to say that 'cause I was busy and kept my nose to the grindstone, somehow . . . I was *wicked* . . . when some of the lazy blokes, idlin' away time in town—'n money their fam'bly sore needed—would've mayhap felt good about their lot, for all *they* did was rest seven days a week!"

Brad chuckled. "Well, iffen that ain't the ways of the world for you, Lemont Gartner. And right here 'n now, I want to offer you a sincere apology if I was ever one to casually pass on that old, worn-out remark to you."

"Me too!" Lizzie added. "I've had that sentiment flung at me more'n a time or two, also, 'n thought *I* was the only one that felt plumb prickly over hearin' it!"

"But it's actually true," Billy countered, his tone reflective. "When you view it in the right time frame—that is, comparing our time down here and the Lord's time in paradise. There *ain't* rest for the wicked, be assured . . . *not then*. Not ever. . . ."

Billy quoted several Scriptures that depicted everlasting torment for those who defiantly rebelled against the Lord and went to their deaths refusing to repent.

Lizzie shuddered at the specter of what eternal damnation represented.

"Sometimes, William LeFave, I think you're a man with a callin'!" Lizzie marveled, hugging him. "Ain't his wisdom just swell?"

"Bill's a bright young fellow, all right," Brad said, "but I have thought some of the wisdom he's been favorin' us with has been the Holy Spirit sheddin' light on our daily lives 'n ever'day instances."

"Ever feel called to the pulpit, Will?" Lemont asked. "I had a cousin was a circuit-ridin' preacher down in Tennessee."

"Can't say that I have," Billy admitted. "At the moment, I'm feeling more led to be a steamboat captain than anything."

"A steamboat captain!" Lizzie and Brad cried in unison, surprised.

"There's a need," Billy replied, shrugging.

"And you're fit to bust with wantin' to tell us all about it," Lizzie teased, quickening her steps. She looped her elbow through the arm of Serenity, who had finally managed to stop crying.

"I brought some fresh-baked cookies along, Will. Serenity and I'll put coffee on, and you can tell us about your plans while we rest up from the trip and prepare to spend the night before departin' for town in the morning!"

"Aye, aye," Billy said, winking at Brad as he snapped off a mock salute to Lizzie.

"We'd best do as Liz says, Son, or she'll consider us mutinous and make us walk the gangplank for sure! Steamboatin', hmmmm? Now that's a downright interestin' prospect. . . ."

Minneapolis–St. Paul, Minnesota

En route to the Twin Cities on the noisy, sooty, clattery train, Lolly was helpless not to gawk around her. It was the first time in all of her years that she'd boarded a train, but she took it in stride, aware that it was an event meant to be.

Her fingers fairly itched to reach into her reticule for a deck of tarot cards and be comforted by the sight of their grilled backs, if only for the sheer relief found in holding them in her grip and trusting that all the answers in the world were contained within the deck.

The cards that Lolly was sorely tempted to withdraw were her own, since the ones bequeathed to her by Grandma Rava were packed away with the heirloom crystal ball and were not as readily available.

She considered going ahead with her desires, until she concluded that too many of the passengers aboard with her resembled the townspeople in Redwing who'd decried her as a witch. The comfort that she might receive, she decided, was not worth the risk of having aghast strangers screaming, "Witch . . . witch!" and perhaps causing the aging, red-faced, gray-haired, amply bellied conductor to actually wrest her from the train in the middle of nowhere and abandon her there to appease the majority of the paying clientele.

Lolly contented herself that after she alighted from the train, the first thing she'd do would be to find a secluded spot—perhaps in a public park or other area where she could wander off by herself and remain undisturbed—so that she could consult her various objects of wisdom.

She had no money.

She had no food.

She had no place to stay.

She had no one to turn to.

All she had were her earthly possessions. . . .

Her practical experience with the circus. . . .

And the thrilling—and sometimes chilling—knowledge that she was the Chosen of the Ravachek family . . . and that fame and fortune would be hers. . . .

With such thoughts foremost in her mind, Lolly felt almost lightheartedly optimistic when she departed the train. She smiled pleasantly at several people, who returned the gesture friendly enough after what she recognized as a moment's hesitation.

She looked like a gypsy, she realized, but it couldn't be helped, for that's what she was. And if telling fortunes for a living was her life's destination, there was no harm in appearing to be what she truly was.

Thirty minutes after lugging her valise from the train and walking sufficiently to ease the kinks from her spine, Lolly found a secluded area. It wasn't a park. It appeared to be the private corner of a wealthy person's estate. Lolly glanced around, contented herself that no one observed her, and a minute later she was secreted within a wildwood of shrubbery as private as a deep timber, even as she was in the midst of a sprawling big city.

Although she was weary, she shuffled the cards, began to lay them out, and with delight read the clues and signs for her future.

It was good. Very, very good!

She almost gasped with excitement at what was revealed. No wonder at times—not when she consulted it regarding others but when she looked into it in an effort to forecast her own fate—the crystal ball had seemed murky to her!

Clearly, according to the tarot cards, a break with her family was necessary that she could become the person she was meant to be in her own right.

The sun was slanting lower, and Lolly sensed that it would only be frustrating to try to peer into the crystal ball to align what she discovered there with what she knew via the cards.

Better to fall asleep thinking sweet and successful thoughts, she realized as she snuggled against the lush grass beneath the juniper boughs that blanketed over her, than to lie awake, too exhausted to sleep, frustrated by murky, ominously conflicting messages from the crystal ball.

Before long, even with her stomach rumbling, Lolly fell asleep. She rested well and dreamed beautiful dreams, which, when she awoke, comforted and inspired her.

Postdawn sunlight was filtering through the juniper boughs when Lolita awakened and could see well enough to find her crystal ball and place it strategically before her. She began to focus sharply, peering into it, prepared to wait however long it took.

But that morning, the ball was as cooperative as in the recent past it had been opaquely vague of all meaning for her.

At times, Lolly's breath was pent, so excited was she by the wondrous flashes and illuminations that were vivid within the crystal ball.

For her!

All for her!

She would make lots of money . . .

She would know success . . .

She would have fine clothes . . .

She would not ever have to work hard . . .

She would live in a beautiful area—an area of pine trees, clear indigo skies, and breathtakingly beautiful beaches lapped at by a sea that seemed to stretch on forever . . .

She saw a train . . .

A long journey . . .

A depot . . .

She strained, squinting, as she peered into the crystal ball to make out the lettering on the building.

W-I-L-L-I- . . .

But the white-and-black sign attached to the mustard yellow and maroon clapboard depot was in need of paint, and it was difficult to make out the last letters, a faint A-M-S.

And marriage!

She saw marriage, just as she had in the cards, but no name and no face were revealed to her.

"This is amazing . . .," Lolly breathed to herself.

A shiver of delight rippled through her, causing goose bumps to course over her tawny flesh, even though the early summer day was already growing warmly humid.

Lolly might have thought that what she was seeing in the ball was only the actions of an overzealous imagination embroidering appealing details into what the cards had revealed the previous evening, but there were too many fresh aspects and facets of which she'd been unaware. And they dovetailed beautifully, logically, and most wondrously with what hints she'd already been given to help her seek and find her destiny!

From the crystal ball's instructions, she knew that she was to work for a season before setting out to fulfill her destiny.

Suddenly all fear left her heart. As she wedged back out of her hiding place, shaking juniper needles from her gypsy hair and clothing, she could've burst into song over such relieved happiness.

There was nothing to fear in her future!

She wouldn't have to hunt for work and risk rude and disgruntled people screaming, "Witch! Witch!" in her face.

Work would find her—and soon—for the cards and ball had both promised that she'd never know hunger, she'd never know want, and she'd be as accepted by people as she could be!

As she walked down the street, Lolly suddenly laughed.

She wondered if Zita had cast a curse upon her. She'd been told by Grandma Rava, Zita, and her father that one had to be most careful in casting a curse, because if it wasn't done just exactly right—or if the other person's power was greater—then instead of the curse going out to the marked individual, the curse could fling back in one's face so one could live out the prescribed misery oneself.

Had Zita cast a curse at her?

Only to have it return to herself?

Knowing Zita, Lolly didn't doubt that the shrew might've considered it, perhaps even done it. There was bad blood between them, Lolly knew, and she had a sudden desire to punish her mean-mouthed, manipulating magpie-of-an-aunt for all the misery that had accumulated over the many years.

But the desire was not strong enough for such a novice in the ways of the dark arts to consider working a curse, lest she do it wrong. Then she would risk it returning to her—and through her own actions, she would spoil the destiny that was at the moment hers to claim.

chapter

6

Minneapolis–St. Paul, Minnesota

LOLLY HAD FAITH in the tarot card and crystal ball predictions. She'd seen them accurate more times than she could recall seeing them wrong, dating back in time to when she was just learning how to walk and talk.

But she was also aware that there were times when the dark spirits were purposely misleading, deceptive, even obnoxious, or impishly told half-truths that, Grandma Rava had sometimes sighed, were "worse than full-fledged lies. . . ."

But by and large, Lolly trusted in her occultic paraphernalia and inherited abilities, as did the clients—referred to in the professional fortune-telling realm as "the fools"—who sought paid consultations.

Lolly considered herself a bright and articulate woman, deceptively well educated for a girl with no formal schooling, so she didn't mind casting herself as the "fool" in order to consult the otherworldly entities so that they might reveal their hidden wisdom. Mystical secrets regarding the past, the present, and the future, that—when revealed and heeded— assured Lolly she might live her life more perfectly in her day-to-day existence.

Even so, Lolly had not expected the opportunity for employment that the tarot cards had predicted to arise as quickly as it did.

She was making her way along the streets, traversing one that was very crowded with what appeared to be rush-hour pedestrian traffic.

A vivaciously dressed woman in a frilly, flouncy dress, with dazzling parasol to match, stumbled as her high-heeled slipper caught in a crack in the sidewalk. She pitched forward, and the shiny, filigreed metal point on her parasol jabbed toward Lolly like a bayonet.

Lolly leaped out of the way but not quite quickly enough, for the little spear of metal penetrated her worn reticule. As she abruptly swerved, it knifed through the threadbare fabric. Her comb, hairbrush—and deck of tarot cards—plunked to the pavement at their feet as the beautiful, artfully coifed and cosmeticized woman struggled to regain her footing.

"I'm so sorry, miss!" the pretty girl cried, grasping Lolly's forearm. "Did I hurt you?"

"No. Only my reticule."

The well-dressed woman regarded it. Even a fool could have known that it was the only one that Lolly owned. Now it was ruined.

"It was my clumsiness, so the least I can do, in addition to tendering my apologies, is to make good on your loss. I have any number of handbags and reticules. If you don't mind accompanying me to my quarters—I'll allow you to replace it with the pick of my possessions."

With a flashing thought, Lolly recalled what nimble fingers her brother Boris possessed, and she considered that if the woman's attention could be drawn away, she might be able to relieve her of a few expensive trinkets to sell at a pawnshop, in addition to a replacement reticule.

Lolly said nothing, for she was too busy trying to stuff her deck of cards into the waistband of her colorful skirt so that she wouldn't risk having them fall undetected from the gash in her reticule and become lost.

"Oh . . . tarot cards!"

The woman gave a little squeal of excitement when she recognized the design on the back of the cards.

"Yes . . .," Lolly casually acknowledged.

"Can you read them?" the woman inquired, then didn't wait for an answer, for she saw how worn the deck was. "Obviously, you can."

"I'm very good," Lolly replied.

There was no braggadocio, only fact, in her tone of voice.

"We shall see! My name is Katrina—but everyone calls me Kitty. And you might be?. . ."

"Lolita. But my friends call me Lolly."

Last names were unimportant to either woman.

They made idle chitchat as they walked along. Kitty slowed as they neared a rather noisy but well-maintained saloon.

"This is where I work. Some girls and I live upstairs." Kitty was a bit apologetic, as if giving Lolly some kind of warning, but the gypsy girl was nonplussed. She regarded the establishment with mere interest and had no hesitancies about passing through the doorway of the Lucky Lady Saloon. "Welcome to our prosperous little den of iniquity! C'mon upstairs, hon. We'll replace your reticule."

When they reached her room, Kitty opened up one of many trunks. Enclosed inside were more handbags and shoes than Lolly had ever seen, except in store windows as she passed by on the street. "Take your time. And take your pick," Kitty generously offered.

Lolly looked at the dazzling colors, styles, leathers, fabrics, and her mind was aswirl. She could pick but one—and it was her heart's desire to have a trunk of her own as lushly lavish. She loved beauty—but searched for something solid and functional.

Finally she made her choice.

"It's yours," Kitty affirmed.

"Thank you," Lolly politely replied.

"It is I who should thank you," Kitty said, smiling warmly, "for being such a well-bred gentlewoman about it all and not purposely making me feel worse about it than I already did."

After having been harangued and called a witch—and following a lifetime spent with the serpent-tongued Aunt Zita—Lolly thought that Kitty's words were among the kindest she could remember hearing. She wanted to repay the older woman's kindness, but she had nothing to give.

Except!. . .

"Would you like me to read your fortune?"

"Oh . . . yes! Would you?!"

"For free, of course," Lolly offered.

"I'd be glad to pay you," Kitty said.

"I wouldn't think of accepting it. You've treated me with such kindness—me, a stranger just arrived in this city."

"Very well," Kitty agreed. "Just tell me what to do! This is so exciting!"

They seated themselves at a small dressing table that Kitty had unceremoniously cleared of perfume bottles, lipstick pots, rouge and powder containers, by sweeping them into a willow clothes basket she'd upended onto an ornate little sofa.

"Shuffle the cards, please . . .," Lolly murmured.

Kitty did it—and poorly, but it mattered not.

In Lolly's familiar hands, the same cards took on a life of their own. Then she began to precisely lay them out—slowly voicing what she saw aligned for her identification and transmission to the beautiful "fool" seated across the vanity table and hanging on every utterance with bated breath.

"You're incredible!" Kitty cried, her face flushed with astonishment. "It's amazing, that's what it is! Why, you told me things that I've never told anyone in my life. You couldn't have known. I've never seen you before. You just got into town. You know not only a few things—you seem to know everything. The way you know so much about my past—it really gives me hope about the future too!"

"Well, I'd better go," Lolly eventually said, helpless not to feel sad, especially when she considered that she still had nowhere to go and no money to take her there.

"I have to go to work, too," Kitty said. "I'll walk you to the street."

Downstairs, the bargirls were appearing to go to work. They greeted Kitty, looked at Lolly with curious stares, which departed as soon as Kitty explained that Lolly was a tremendously talented fortune-teller.

"Oh . . . do you have a minute to tell mine?" one wheedled.

"Me too!" another cried.

"I've always wanted to have someone read my palm or something."

Kitty took control and clapped her hands for the women's attention.

"Lolly doesn't just give her services away, although my reading was for free. That's because we're friends. I'm sure that perhaps Lolita can be persuaded to find the time to do readings, but she must not be expected to do it for free for you just because she's my friend. We're all working girls. We know that it takes money to get along in this world on our own. So if you want Lolly to read your fortunes, then prepare to break loose with some of your hard-earned cash so that she can use it to support herself!"

"Can we?" Lolly asked softly. "I mean, do we have the time? Mustn't you all go to work?"

Kitty piffled her fingers. "The barkeep's not even here yet."

"We could use this private table right over here!" another handsome woman who was employed by the Lucky Lady Saloon suggested.

A half hour later Lolly was still reading fortunes, when the paunchy, balding, florid-faced barkeep entered, his eyebrows shooting up in alarm when he saw the cluster of activity.

"What's going on, girls?" he demanded.

"A gypsy girl is reading our fortunes!"

"Oh, yeah?" he replied, interest apparent in his tone. He sauntered over to where Lolly was busy with a "fool." "I wonder if she'd do mine?. . ."

"Perhaps when she has time," Kitty said. "I think I'd like to try my hand at this fortune-telling art," she said, winking broadly at the other girls as the sweating barkeeper sat down at a vacant table across from her and opened his palm.

"Practice on me," he agreeably invited, winking, apparently not taking it seriously.

Kitty frowned, then stared with seriousness. "You are a fool . . . and will miss many golden opportunities . . . if you do not make arrangements for Lolita to be the Know-Your-Luck-Before-You-Live-It Lady at the Lucky Lady Saloon."

The barkeep looked up, appeared amazed, seemed to see into his own future and discover rich potential. He called across to Lolly.

"Hey, girlie! Kitty's right! I'm offerin' you a job."

" . . . And I'm accepting!. . ."

"We'll talk about money when you're done with what you're doing."

Lolly fixed him with a sharp stare, focused in on him very intently, then laughed.

"I already know what you're offering," she said.

He didn't for a moment doubt that it was somehow true.

"And I know the terms I have in mind. . . ."

The barkeep groaned.

"And that you *will* accept," she teased.

Which, within twenty minutes, is exactly what he did, wondering all the while how she could have actually known the very unspoken thoughts that had swirled through his mind.

The first week of her alliance with the Lucky Lady, she was to be free to keep the totality of her earnings, and after that she'd pay a commission of ten percent of her earnings, plus room and board.

The cards and ball had been right. She would become rich and famous—and perhaps sooner than she'd ever dreamed.

Then she might one day find herself interested in fulfilling more of her destiny: matrimony. To a man in a town called Williams. . . .

Grant Hotel
Williams, Minnesota

"You're serious as a heart attack about this steamboat thing, ain't ya, Will?" Lizzie asked as he sat in the hotel kitchen and enjoyed a steaming cup of coffee, and cookies fresh from the oven.

"Sure am, Ma."

"Thought mayhap you was joshin' us all that night out at the cabin when you mentioned it. It caught us all by surprise."

"I see a good future for it," Billy said. "Already there are a few commercial fishermen plying the lake, harvesting fish in our country's water and having good catches when they've passed into the Canadian territory."

"That's what I've heard tell."

"We've got the train, and it's dandy for transporting people and cargo where the tracks are laid. But there are places up in Canada, and out on the lake, that won't ever have roads or railways to link them up with others. The way I see it, as folks move to these parts, they'll need steamship passage to take them and their goods and possessions to some of the places they want to go."

"And if such a mode of travel is available, it'll encourage folks indwelt with the pioneer spirit to forge on."

"Exactly!" Billy said.

Lizzie gave a low whistle. "Sounds to me like that'll take a powerful lot o' jack."

" . . . I know," Billy said, his tone suddenly dismal. "And I don't have it."

"Alas, neither do we," Lizzie sighed, "although iffen there's some way we can help you—don't you hesitate to ask!"

"I'll appreciate prayers, Ma," Billy said.

"That goes without mention, Son. You'll have them always."

"I'm going to make an appointment with the president of the bank in Baudette," Billy said. "Sure do wisht we had our own bank in Williams, where I'm known."

"Homer Ames promised to work on that," Lizzie said. "And he's a man of his word. I know he'd help you, Son, iffen you'd send him a telegram."

"I'd rather make it on my own merit, Ma, 'n not give anyone a chance to claim Homer paid me special favor, or—"

"I understand," Lizzie murmured.

"So! I'll be taking the train over one of these first days. If I don't get back in time to head out to my property, I'd appreciate it if you'd put me up for the night."

Lizzie gave him a hug. "That too goes without askin', Son. You're fam'bly. Always will be. Even if . . ."—she swallowed hard and tried to keep her voice unfathomable—"you find yourself another woman to love and decide to marry up again."

Billy made a grunt into his coffee.

Lizzie didn't ask him to repeat it.

"It ain't good for a man to be alone," she softly pointed out.

Billy said nothing.

Neither did Lizzie.

At that moment, Lizzie wondered if they were both thinking about Way-Say-Com-a-Gouk. Her name meant "Far Away Sky," but these days, looking at her woman-to-woman and knowing what the sighs, secret smiles, blushes, and shy excitement really meant, Lizzie had thought in her own mind that "Stars in Her Eyes" would be every bit as appropriate for their beloved Serenity.

Serenity . . . the beautiful, dainty Chippewa Indian maiden who had finally ceased saying, "I'm sorry!" to the handsome Billy LeFave only after the strapping Frenchman sternly ordered the apologies to end. . . .

Minneapolis, Minnesota

Although Lolly, born into a family with an itinerant spirit, was happy at the Lucky Lady Saloon—and there was no doubt that it was extremely profitable to sit at a corner table and give consultations, secreting her earnings away while she paid the establishment a commission fee on her daily wages— she found herself a victim of a strange discontent.

At different times, she met men at the saloon, and their

interest in her was apparent, but she knew that they were not, any of them, meant for her.

One bargirl left, preparing to marry a gent, soon after Lolly had taken up residence above the saloon. Now another was engaged, causing all of the girls to have stars in their eyes and matrimony on their minds.

Lolly considered herself "rich and famous" by her own measure, although she knew that the Astors, Rockefellers, and Vanderbilts would laugh her to shame at the very idea.

Nonetheless, she had more money than she'd seen together in one place, she possessed new and stylish clothing, she had her same dark good looks, enhanced now by outfits that Kitty had helped her to select, and she was well known in the Twin Cities for her psychic abilities. What she didn't have and wanted—in addition to her quickly won fame, her bank account, and her silk bag containing a cache of gold coins— was a handsome man . . . love . . . matrimony . . . and a wonderful existence in a train town named Williams.

That was her destiny.

And each day she spent at the saloon felt like a long and disappointing detour.

Already she possessed what the cards and crystal ball had offered as their edicts, given for her knowledge and discernment so that she could take action.

With that in mind, Lolly located a bulletin brimming with classified advertising, then sipped coffee, smoked cheroots, and pored over the listings.

Her touch on the newspaper advertisements—using her psychometric abilities—narrowed the list down to three offices. She made note of them but added two more, for a total of five marriage broker businesses, just to be safe.

She believed in the cards' and ball's powers.

She would not be disappointed.

There *would* be a Williams, Minnesota.

And there *would* be a gentleman who'd ordered a mail-order bride from one of the three establishments.

Walking in, inquiring about marrying a man from Williams, would be her key. Undoubtedly, the marriage broker would be startled by her unexpected, unpredictable knowledge.

But in her heart of hearts, she would then *know* . . . for the crystal ball had said it was so. . . .

It was definitely going to be a love meant to be!

chapter
7

Shantytown

FOND OF THAD, as if he were one of her own brood, Amelia Jackson gave him a gentle pat on the shoulder as he sat at the rickety table, which was bare save for the coal oil lantern that she'd lit and placed before him, giving unspoken blessing that the precious kerosene was his to use as he saw fit—as was the foolscap paper and a stubby length of pencil that Thad meticulously sharpened with a pocketknife that Amos kept well whetted.

Amelia cleared her throat and sank into the wobbly chair across from Thad.

"Yo' goin' ter leave us—ain't yo'?"

There was pain in her eyes. But Thad couldn't lie.

"Yes'm. I . . . have . . . to. . . ."

"Ah knows dat. . . . Go to yo' mammy, Son. Lawsy but she be happy ter set eyes on yo'!"

Thad nodded. "I reckon. I hope so. . . ."

"She be as happy as Ah be missin' yo'."

"I'll miss the Jacksons, that's for sure."

"Stay in touch, won't yo'?"

"Sure thing," Thad replied. "I'll write. And when I'm able, I'll send some money to help out and repay you for all the kindness and Christian charity you've shown me. Until you're better repaid—all I can say is—thanks!"

Amelia smiled and nodded.

"How soon yo' be leavin'?" she softly inquired.

Thad gave a heavy sigh. "Travelin' costs money. And that's one thing I don't have, 'n it'll take me a while to get."

"Travelin' don' allus have ter cost money," Amelia pointed out. She cocked her head and listened to the moan of a barge on the Mississippi not more than a few stone's throws away. "Sign you on with a barge company. Yo' work for dem, dey pays yo', 'n yo' get where yo' wantin' ter go dat much faster!"

Thad wondered why he hadn't thought of it himself.

Then he realized it was because he hadn't been able to do much thinking for a long, long time. What memories had come back he'd quickly jotted down on paper, writing tiny so as not to waste space. He was relieved that the events were recorded, for he no longer trusted the mind that had so long betrayed him when a horrible darkness had overtaken it until the amazing light of an old, well-loved hymn had swept the darkness away.

"I'll never forget you, Amelia," Thad said. "And I will stay in touch. Iffen you don't mind, I'd like to think of you as 'Ma.' My second mama."

Amelia grinned. Her strong, dark grip lay across his smoothly tanned white skin. "Ah'd like dat a pow'rful lot!"

"I'd be hard-pressed to venture as to who gives the best rendition of 'Amazing Grace,' Ma," Thad teased. "And iffen you and my mama ever meet, instead of havin' competition, I think y'all had better settle for singin' a duet."

"Dat may happen, Son," Amelia assured, "iffen not in dis here world, sho' nuff it'll happen in de next!"

St. Louis, Missouri

"Dinner was lovely," Nanette Kelly thanked her host, "but

if you don't mind, I've some correspondence to catch up on, and I need to retire."

"Go ahead, and bless you, child. You must get sufficient rest," the elderly widow reminded. "Doing the Lord's work can be a strenuous labor."

Nanette smiled. She gave the woman a quick hug. "Thank you for being so understanding."

Up in her room, Nanette bathed, retired into her nightgown, withdrew several sheets of paper, and sat at the quaint little writing desk in the corner of what had been her quarters for the past two nights.

After knowing what it was to have a home at Mrs. Poindexter's boardinghouse, this transient lifestyle seemed strange, but Nanette adjusted to it. She contented herself that the Lord would provide for her needs and that whatever quarters she received—whether luxurious or spartan—it was his choice, and she gratefully accepted.

Knowing that she would be leaving St. Louis in the morning—going northward again to be met by a pastor who was holding a series of tent meetings—and aware that she would be extremely busy, Nanette realized that she needed to take what moments she could find and write to Lizzie Mathews that very night, or another opportunity might not present itself for longer than Nanette would approve.

Dear Lizzie, she wrote, feeling pleased that their relationship had grown from "Dear Mrs. Mathews" and "Dear Miss Kelly" to first-name business after her second letter. That letter had taken supreme courage to write. In it Nanette had chronicled how she and Nick had come to meet Thad, how he'd joined them, how a relationship had grown between Nanette and Thad, and how this had provoked such animosity in Nick that—she'd concluded, although she hadn't been present to witness the altercation—he shot Thad, who fell into the Mississippi River, in gator territory.

As she wrote the lines and copied Thad's last written words to her so that they could edify his mother, she knew that somehow her admission had paved the way for peace for Lizzie, a peace even unto forgiveness for Nanette's part in her son's demise. It was, Nanette realized, because she and Lizzie both loved the same Savior—and also had loved the same person, Thad Childers—that there would forever be a bond between them, beyond mere forgiven and forgiving.

My travels have been everything I've hoped for and more. The Lord is gracious in his bounty, and there's pleasure in laboring as I know I am meant to serve.

Weather has been fit here in the central Mississippi Valley. Quite perfect for the many tent meetings at which I now find myself, in addition to testifying in word and song at various churches in towns and villages.

As I'm sure you had surmised, I've met many, many wonderful people from all walks of life. Yet we're all united in Jesus Christ. I now have happiness I never real- ized existed. There is joy in witnessing to people who used to live as I did and in giving them assurance that God loves them too and in seeing the changes wrought in their lives when they accept him.

I will be venturing on again tomorrow. So many of the wonderful pastors I've been blessed to meet have desired to telegraph or write to peers—and always, always it seems to be leading me farther north!

It is my hope that it is the Lord's will that one day you and I can meet. I would love that. And to meet the wonderful people in your little town, strangers to me, I know, but who, from the warmth and wit of your letters, Lizzie, I feel as if I already know.

How happy you must be to have Mr. Gartner there to join you. He sounds like a wonderful fellow. I missed having a nice grandpa (or any grandfather that I can recall), so I am sure your grown children cherish him in a special place in their hearts.

I hope that all is going well with you. I was sorry to learn that you'd suffered through such a variety of illness and difficulties. We have to learn to accept the painful with the pleasant, for there's a godly purpose in all.

Thank you so much for writing, Lizzie. I do so look forward to arriving at various destinations—in hope there will be friendly correspondence awaiting me. And it's always a treat to go to a post office and ask for general delivery mail to make me feel closer to those that I've left behind in order to spread the Gospel.

Thank you for your prayers and the promise of more. I greatly appreciate the prayer covering from my church friends. I know that it helps immensely in protecting and strengthening me. Rest assured that I will remember you and yours in my talks with the Lord.

Fondly,
Nanette Kelly

Nanette paused, reread what she had written, addressed an envelope, affixed a stamp, and then positioned the final sheet of the letter in front of herself, adding:

P.S.: If it is inconvenient or you would prefer not to have me travel to Williams to visit, please inform me quickly so I can make other plans. (And know that whatever your choice, there will be no bad feelings. NK)

With that, Nanette folded the papers, sealed the envelope, and after depositing it in a drop box en route to her ship, put it from her mind.

Williams, Minnesota

"Any mail, darlin'?" Lizzie called out to Brad when she heard him return from Lundsten's Mercantile, where the post office was also housed.

"A few things."

"Hopefully something of interest."

"A thick letter from your friend Nan."

"Well! That's a treat. Honey, would you mind stirrin' the gravy so's I can rest over a cup of coffee and read her note straightaway?"

"Be glad to, Liz. You don't even have to ask . . .," Brad said, giving her a fond pat.

He was carefully stirring the thickening gravy with a long-handled wooden spoon when Lizzie let out a whoop.

"What's wrong, Liz?!"

"Ain't nothin' wrong—but sure could be right! Miss Nanette says she might come to visit iffen it's all right with us. I have a hunch that Pastor Edgerton would love havin' her bless us with song at our services while she's in town. I know *I* would."

"Same here."

Lizzie leaped to her feet. "I'll take over with that wooden spoon, darlin', and ask if you'd do me the special favor of run-nin' back over to the post office and buyin' me a penny post-card. Nan's waitin' on an answer—and I won't take time to turn it into a decent-length letter. A postcard's quicker."

Brad grinned and held on to the spoon even as Lizzie reached to take it. "I think this time I'll stay right where I am." But with his other hand, he was digging in his pocket for change. "Here you go, honey. Take a break and go to the post office yourself. It's a purty day out there, 'n that way you can buy the card, write the message, and post it, all at the same time!"

Moline, Illinois

Nanette Kelly approached the busy window clerk at the downtown post office.

"He'p you, miss?" he inquired.

"Uh . . . yes. My name is Nanette Kelly, and I was wondering if you have some mail being held for me here in your general delivery section."

"I'll go have a quick look-see and find out," he said.

A moment later he returned with a small sheaf in his hand.

"Sure do, miss. And here it is!"

"Thank you so much!" Nanette said.

When she got into the street and paused long enough to riffle through her assortment of mail, she felt almost wilted with relief and yet buoyed with what seemed nigh on uncontainable joy.

"Thank you, Lord!" she whispered, and tears of relieved joy filmed her eyes.

Over and over she looked at the postcard from Lizzie Mathews. Short and to the point but conveying so, so much.

Dear Nan,

Y'all come to Williams just as soon as you can. We'll put an extra plate on the table, turn down the sheets on a spare bed, and look forward to you staying with us for as long as you're able and the Good Lord allows.

Love,

Lizzie Mathews (and family and friends)

Minneapolis–St. Paul, Minnesota

"My, don't you look gorgeous this morning!" Kitty said, sleepily opening an eye to see Lolly all dolled up in her finest outfit, hat in place, prepared to depart. "You're as dressed up as Astor's horse!"

"That I am!"

Kitty yawned. "What are you planning on doing at this unearthly hour, pray tell?"

"Our hours certainly aren't everyone's hours," Lolly mysteriously pointed out. "And I have business to attend to."

"Really? What kind of business?"

"Storming and conquering the matrimonial industry!"

"Do tell!" Kitty breathed, her eyes widening in shock, for she and all the rest of the girls regularly had to dodge the sincere and frequently overzealous proposals of drunken mankind sodden with strong drink and soppy with misplaced affection. "Who is the lucky man?"

Lolly met her eyes. "I have no idea. That's what I'm setting out to discover."

"You're confusing me," Kitty complained. "It's too early in the morning to expect me to think well. . . ."

"I'll be marrying someone from Williams, Minnesota."

Kitty frowned. "I've never heard of the place."

"Neither had I."

" . . . Does it exist?"

"Indeed it does!"

Lolly explained what she'd learned about the place from what the ticket agent at the train depot was able to tell her . . . and what little she knew of the area from the crystal ball's revelations.

"A man from Williams has ordered a wife from a marriage broker."

"And you're the merchandise guaranteed to meet his satisfaction?"

"I am. So it's merely a matter of appearing at the right marriage broker's, presenting myself, solving his problem, and going forth to meet my fate."

"You're some girl," Kitty said, shaking her tousled hair, then wearily falling back against the pillow. "There's never a dull moment when you're around. It seems that you attract weird situations the way a magnet draws iron filings."

" . . . Really?" Lolly responded.

Kitty grinned, then playfully threw a pillow at her younger friend.

"Don't take offense, darling," she said. "Trust me—oddity becomes you! You're such a treat to know. Marvelous. Mysterious. Mystical. Marriageable too. Some unknown fellow is in for a delight."

"I hope so."

"But tell me, Lolly, how will you stand it? And how will he stand it? Heavens, I should think it would be unbearable for you to know what he's thinking—and for him to know that you know the secrets of his mind. He could keep nothing from you! Not even his most private thoughts."

"Surely the ball has revealed to me the man who can endure such a life with me," Lolly said. She waggled her fingers, blew a good-bye kiss in Kitty's direction, and confidently walked out the door.

She was feeling less sure of herself after traveling to three of the five marriage brokers, walking in, announcing, "I wish to marry a fellow from Williams, Minnesota, who applied for a wife," and having the staffers at the establishments look at her as if she were absolutely daft.

They'd never heard of the place.

Nor had they received any applications from such a town.

By the time Lolly approached the fourth business, her confidence was shaken and her demeanor was more chastened. Her initial introduction displayed it.

"Good day. I know that this will probably seem like your most unusual request of the day, but could you tell me if you have received an application from a gentleman in Williams, Minnesota, seeking a bride?"

After three strikeouts, Lolly was prepared to be disappointed a fourth time, but then trusted she'd know success at the fifth establishment. Her faith in the occult was not shaken, for she reminded herself that sometimes the spirits were playful, at other times obnoxiously malicious, seeming to delight in making unnecessary and time-consuming work for those serious about following their wise predictions.

Lolly was bracing herself for a response like those she'd suffered through three times earlier that day.

"Williams? You *did* say *Williams?*"

Lolly drew a quick breath. "I most certainly did."

"I don't even have to look," the gentleman said. "We're now familiar with the town, for we did receive an application and it left us with a quandary. It's terribly far away, in a very remote area, and we couldn't think of anyone presently in our listings who'd even dream of traveling that far and living in such a region, even if her intended had the appearance of Adonis and the wealth of King Tut!"

"Undoubtedly, I'm your woman!" Lolly quietly said.

The young gentleman looked at her as if she'd certainly fill an order he might file, but he reached for a sheet of paper.

Not all men's tastes ran the same when it came to feminine pulchritude.

"Let me consult the paperwork."

"Don't worry," Lolly said, "I'll exactingly match his desires."

The man scanned the sheet—and his mouth dropped open.

"That you do!" He gave Lolly a queer look. "Is this some kind of a joke? A test? To see if we're a bona fide and legitimate concern, or—"

"I've never been more serious," Lolly said. "Now, if you will, can you make the matrimonial arrangements?"

"With pleasure!" the man said, smiling broadly as he offered her a chair and withdrew more paperwork, went over the contracts, explained the recompense that she would receive and all the surrounding details of which she must be aware.

"Any questions?" the clerk asked when everything was in order and the papers signed.

"None that you can answer," Lolly said.

And if any arose in her mind, she had only to consult her crystal ball and get the reponses that she would need.

Williams, Minnesota

"William LeFave, you're absolutely gorgeous!" Lizzie Mathews cried when he came down the curving staircase of the Grant Hotel, dressed in a dark suit and handsomely decked out in a cravat, with a gold pocket watch artfully draped, a silk handkerchief in his breast pocket, his shoes shined and his spats brilliant white.

"Thank you, Ma," he said. "I . . . feel rather . . . ridiculous! I don't feel myself in borrowed clothing!"

"Well, you look as if those duds were made for you

instead of for Luke and Marc, bless their hearts! You look *very* distinguished."

"I wish I felt as distinguished," he said.

"Cup of coffee?" Lizzie suggested.

"With gratitude," Billy said and seemed to almost wilt into the kitchen chair Lizzie gestured toward. She got two mugs of coffee. She was ready to take a break—and sensed that Will could use a bit of encouragement.

"Nervous, are you?"

"You have to ask?" he answered her question with one of his own, chuckling.

"Almost as nervous as you were the day you made up your mind to ask my Harmony to marry you?" Lizzie teased.

"This's almost as hard as that was," Billy joined her in laughter. "But not quite."

"You were successful with Harmony, and Lord knows she was a shrewd and cautious woman. God willing, you'll be every bit as successful with the banker in Baudette."

"I hope so. . . ."

"You believe in yourself and believe and trust in your Creator, Will—and that's a pretty impressive combination. I believe in you, too, as do a lot of others."

" . . . But I have no money."

"That doesn't have to stop you."

"But I'm afraid it *can* stop me." Billy sighed. "You know how it is—the rich get richer and the poor tend to get poorer. Bankers don't want to lend people without money any capital— and if you've got such capital that you don't need borrowed funds, then they're tripping all over themselves trying to loan you money so you can make more money and they can, too!"

Lizzie laughed. "You're such a wise man, William LeFave! Iffen that banker detects your wisdom and all o' your other attributes—then unless he's a brass-plated fool, he's going to take a risk on what appears to me a sure thing and do business with you!"

"I hope you're right."

"How long's this business trip going to take you?"

"I'm not sure. There are two banks in Baudette, and if the first banker isn't astute enough to see me as you do, Ma, then I'll have to hang around and approach the second. And then I'll also have to wait for an answer, perhaps, for I've gathered that sometimes bankers have to think things over and don't give immediate answers."

"The train'll be here soon, headin' east," Lizzie said, arising and giving Billy a solid hug after he drained his coffee cup. "We'll see ya when we see ya!"

"Hopefully, it'll be soon."

"I'll keep an eye peeled toward each incomin' train from the east, Son. Iffen there's anything we can do—let us know."

chapter

8

Williams, Minnesota

"THIS MUST BE a joke!" Lolly blurted after stepping from the train and almost fainting dead away when the man of her dreams and crystal ball's revelation marched forth to claim her—and proved to be a smelly, living, breathing nightmare!

"Tain't a joke!" he whined. "Ah was serious—m' money in dead earnest!"

Then he gave Lolly an aim-to-please grin, exposing snaggled, brown, and rotting teeth.

Lolly's tawny face blanched pale as clabbered milk before her cheeks became a mottled red that stood out like a fiery rash. For perhaps the first time in her entire life, the gypsy woman was rendered speechless.

"C'mon, girlie!" the fetid-breathed lumberjack encouraged. "Ah'll take you to your new cabin—our cabin!" Gallantly he reached for Lolly's valise.

Instinctively, protectively, she snatched it back.

The lumberjack's rheumy eyes flew open like runaway window shades at the surprising force of the slim girl's strength.

Lolly found her voice. But it was that of an angered feline.

"I have no intention of accompanying you for so much as one step!" she hissed, turning on her heel, marching indignantly along the platform to get away from him.

The drop-mouthed lumberjack staggered a few paces in

her direction, fumblingly reached for her, but missed. With a few quick steps, she was safely out of his grasp, her glare that of a tigress ready to rip him limb from torso. The lumberjack seemed to realize that she was . . . gone forever.

"But I paid good money for you!" he protested. "I bought you! You're mine! We're going to get hitched! Just like the broker arranged—a deal's a deal!"

"I'd sooner marry the Devil himself!" Lolly flared. "I'll marry the likes of you when donkeys talk and fly!"

She dropped her valise to the platform with a clunk, then, casting a wary eye at the lumberjack, she lifted her flouncy skirt in a quick flash of shapely leg and retrieved a respectable wad of greenbacks from a fancy but functional garter.

Rapidly she peeled off bills, disdainfully counting them as they drifted down onto the weather-beaten boards at their feet.

Without pride, the lumberjack dropped to his feet, muttering, cursing, crumpled the bills together, shoved them into his pocket, and took off toward the Black Diamond Saloon to drown his sorrows. Lolly looked around her, knew a harrowing moment of concern over the force with which she'd dropped her luggage, which contained the tools of her occult trade. She was relieved when after giving it a small shake as she hefted it up again, it failed to produce the tinkling sound of broken glass.

Knowing she couldn't stand in the street and that the mosquitoes were too bloodthirsty for her to remain outside, camped under bushes—not that she had any desire, well dressed as she was nowadays—Lolly looked around.

Like a welcoming beacon, the brightly whitewashed, neatly trimmed, well-maintained Grant Hotel caught her eye.

She headed directly for it, grateful that money was no concern, as the crystal ball had assured—even if it had been wrong, or maliciously deceitful, about her matrimonial destiny in a small, remote, seemingly godforsaken town like . . . Williams!

A bell above the entrance doorway letting into the homey lobby of the Grant Hotel clanged. Lizzie looked up to see a wild-haired, expensively dressed, slim, and very pretty woman pausing hesitantly in the foyer.

"C'mon in!" Lizzie welcomed, quickly wiping her hands and abandoning her apron as she went forward to do desk duties.

"Hello . . .," the girl said, her voice quiet, seeming somewhat deflated and a mite bedraggled from her journey.

"Hello there!" Lizzie said, her tone cheerful. "What can I do for you on this fine day?"

" . . . I'm in need of a room. I do hope that you can accommodate me. Yours seems to be the only hotel in town."

"'Tis! But don't worry, we've a room available, and the rates are fair," Lizzie assured, producing a registration form and a lead pencil. "Your name?"

"Lolita Ravachek," Lolly replied, spelling it as well.

"Pretty name for a pretty young woman!"

"Thank you."

"How long will you be stayin' with us?" Lizzie inquired.

"I . . . I don't really . . . know. A while, perhaps . . .," Lolly spoke her confused thoughts out loud. "At least overnight. When's the next train out of town?"

"Depends on which direction you're wantin' to go," Lizzie said, reaching for a train schedule the depot agent had provided to assist her in better serving the town's guests.

"I don't know where I'm meant to go."

"You're plenty welcome to stay with us whilst you allow time to figure out your future, dear."

Lolly's eyes flicked to Lizzie's face, and the young woman

sensed that maybe she'd just met a kindred spirit who knew what it was to plumb and plan her future by various occult mediums available for her understanding and enlightenment.

" . . . The rooms are clean, comfortable, and pleasant to the eye. Iffen you pardon me for seemin' at risk o' braggin', I can assure you that the meals available in the hotel dining room are the finest and most affordable in the area. You'll have privacy if you want it, and company if that's your desire, for often family, townspeople, or other guests can be found in the dining room or in the lobby area."

"That's nice," Lolly said. "But right now I'll appreciate my privacy so that I can figure out my future. With any luck, I'll receive direction very soon over where my fortune lies."

"Timin's a trick sometimes, ain't it? We seek direction, heavens yes, but get impatient waitin' on the answers. Guess it's cause we tend to forget that there's his time 'n our time. We live by a ticktock clock, and he don't."

"Mmmmm," Lolly said, smiling, her murmur noncommittal. She enjoyed Lizzie's welcoming chatter and didn't want it to cease simply because it became clear that she had no idea as to what the woman referred. Perhaps the woman was mentally deranged, Lolly considered, talking about a "he" as if someone else were in the very room with them.

"If you'll pardon me for mayhap seemin' nosy, I can't help wonderin' how in blue blazes you wound up in our little town out in the middle o' nowhere, being as you don't seem certain a'tall that this is where you should be. Nor are you confident of just where you're goin'."

"I—I arrived to keep an appointment."

"Oh. . . ."

"One arranged by a marriage broker."

Lizzie's breath was a quick intake.

"Welcome to Williams, dear. You ain't the first mail-order bride, 'n doubtless you won't be the last. I would've thought that your intended would've met you at the depot. Don't worry. You know how forgetful men can be—'specially bachelor men! When he finally hies into town, he'll find you here easily enough."

Lolly gave a sickly groan and shuddered. "Oh, he was there waiting, all right! That's why I'm *here*."

" . . . There was a problem?"

"I should hope to say!" Lolly said, and her voice flared indignantly at the very thought. "Like I told him: donkeys would fly and talk before I'd marry the likes of him!"

"Don't recollect that I've ever heard tell of donkeys a-flyin'," Lizzie said. "Talkin' donkeys, now, that's another story—'n one I'm familiar with 'n believe, regardin' Balaam back in the book o' Numbers. . . ."

Lolly gave Lizzie a queer stare.

Lizzie detected it but didn't understand the expression.

"Well, dear, you know what's in your heart."

"And as soon as I'm settled in upstairs," Lolly said after she'd paid in advance for her quarters, "I'm going to know what's in the cards for me."

"Goin' to the post office for general delivery, are you?"

Once more, Lolly looked perplexed. "What makes you think that?"

Lizzie shrugged. "You mentioned cards. Silly of me, I s'pose, but I tend to think in terms of postal cards. I don't have any use for poker cards 'n such, so I don't—"

"I can't say that I've ever received much, if any, mail," Lolly said. "I use tarot cards. I find them wonderfully helpful—and I have a real knack for interpreting their meaning. . . . And when it comes to poker, I'm actually quite—"

95

Lizzie didn't even hear the rest of what Lolly said.

Tarot cards!

Lizzie felt herself wilt inwardly.

"If I don't get the answers I need in the cards," Lolly went on blithely, "then I try crystal ball gazing. Although right now I have a bit of a headache coming on, so I'll have to rest up first. I can do psychometry also, as well as—"

Lizzie was appalled.

She was so shocked and shaken over the revelations of the pretty, quite normal-looking young woman that her mind was hopelessly scrambled.

"My key. . . . May I have my key?" Lolly reminded.

"Oh . . . yes. . . ."

"Thank you."

" . . . Do you need any . . .," Lizzie regarded Lolly's bags, suspected what all might be contained within them, and shuddered at the thought of asking any of the Christian men in the house to help her transport them to her quarters.

"No, I don't need any help. I know you're busy in the kitchen," Lolly observed. "I can find the way to my room."

Two minutes later, after lifting lids, methodically stirring through contents in various pots and kettles, Lizzie poured herself a cup of coffee, added cream, and collapsed into a wooden worktable chair, her head in her hands.

"Oh, Lord . . . help us!" she whispered, stunned, stricken.

Brad came in the back door that entered the hotel near the pantry. He set down a bucket of newly harvested vegetables. Usually Lizzie came forward to admire the garden's bounty. This time she did not. Then he heard her groan, the agonizing, whispered fear, and fright settled over him that his beloved Liz was taking ill again. . . .

"Darlin'? What's wrong?"

"Oh, Brad, this is horrible! Abominable, even. And I don't know what to do!"

"Do about what? Liz, you're not making sense—"

Lizzie purposely lowered her voice and shut the door from the kitchen into the dining room. "We've got us a problem—a mighty big problem!"

Brad was helpless not to tense at the news. They'd been through so much already.

" . . . What now?"

"We have a new lodger," Lizzie said. "She just checked in. She looks normal enough, and you wouldn't know iffen she didn't tell you, but—"

"What's the matter with her?" Brad prompted, impatient in his sudden fright.

"Somethin' I've never confronted before—'n don't know how I . . . we . . . are s'posed to deal with it."

"Would you please tell me what's so terrible about this lodger and what this big problem is?"

"To make a long story short, she's . . . she's . . ."

Lizzie groped for the right word.

Soothsayer?

Diviner?

Necromancer?

Seer?

"She's what?"

"She's a witch!"

Brad was thunderstruck, momentarily as speechless as his wife had been.

"Surely she was jestin', Liz. Or you misunderstood her."

"Don't I wish that was the case! But I vow to you, Brad, she was serious as could be—talkin' about her magical cards that she's no doubt upstairs consultin' even as we speak, and then chatterin' on that iffen the cards fail her, then she's pre-pared to set about peerin' into a crystal ball! She also does something she called psy-cho-met-ry, or some such," Lizzie rushed on. "And I am purty sure it don't bear no relation to that highfalutin mathematical trigonometry!"

"Mercy!" Brad gasped, stunned.

"I ain't never had truck with that kind o' thing, an' while I know that we're here to serve the needs of people who require food and shelter . . . I don't know how comfortable I am about seeing to the needs of . . . a *witch*. I didn't know what she was when I rented her quarters to her. . . ."

"It can't be helped," Brad said thoughtfully, although it was apparent that he too was trying to figure out a course of action.

"What're we goin' to do?"

"For the moment, pro'bly the best action is no action. Could be, Liz, that the Lord's sent her into our midst for a reason."

" . . . I suppose that could be. . . ."

"The Good Book admonishes us to love a wretch even as we hate that person's abomination. Hate the sin but love the sinner, y'know."

"That's true enough."

"Then yo' don't think we should march right up the stairs and . . . ask her to go elsewhere?"

"Where'd she go? We can provide lodging and food with-out encouraging her in her occultic ways. Cain't hardly stone the woman. . . ."

"Reckon Jesus sat down with the worst o' sinners and saved them. He didn't condone what they were doin' nor how they were livin'. His example fell on fertile ground, and his capacity to love the sinner while hatin' the sin won people to the Lord that criticism and harsh condemnation wouldn't have in some cases."

"In other words—"

"Until we are certain what the Lord's will is, it's my thought that we shouldn't take any kind of action. Just treat her as we would any other lodger, seein' to it that she's as comfortable as any other guest, while praying for her as we take pains to stand strong in our own faith and convictions, 'n not accidentally open any forbidden doors by gettin' improperly involved in her ways."

"Come to think of it, Brad, it just occurred to me that this could be a sign of the Lord's protection that we *know* what we're dealin' with in the guest upstairs. Why, iffen she hadn't said the few things she did and I hadn't remarked as I did, with it all seemin' so coincidental—we wouldn't have any idea we had a witch in our midst!. . . ."

"Therefore we know to pray for her—and for this town and its people—to bind the forces of the dark spirits that may be present. It's a comfort to dwell on Scripture that assures us that greater is the One who lives within us than the one who roams the world lookin' for souls to devour. . . ."

"I wonder. . . ."

"Wonder what?"

"How such a thing happened to such a pretty and intelligent-seemin' girl. Iffen you didn't know what she is, you pro'bly wouldn't figure it out."

Brad gave a tired shrug and put his arms around Lizzie in a comforting gesture.

"Well, sweetheart, the way I see it is that our mamas and papas raised us up in Christian ways. Some young'uns are raised up by godless people, and they learn godless ways. They tend to naturally follow the same mistaken path as all o' their ancestors, 'til someone shows them a different path that leads to a brand-new life in the Lord Jesus Christ 'n leads them away from an existence spent detourin' aimlessly in darkness 'n devilment."

"Mayhap that's why she's here in Williams," Lizzie said. "We have a strong church community and many people of faith. Perhaps the Lord can use all o' us in his process of savin' her soul, iffen she'll accept him. . . ."

"Or . . ."—Brad paused, seeming thoughtful and almost reluctant to speak—"it could be that instead she's going to be a tool of testin' for the Christians in this town."

"We're going to have to try the spirits, ain't we?"

"As never before, I'm afraid."

"If we remember to resist evil, it will flee from us."

"We'll have to keep in mind that evil oftentimes ain't ugly and repulsive 'n easily recognized. Sometimes it's especially subtle, appealing . . . mayhap even so beautiful that it hardly seems possible it originates from the pits of hell. . . ."

This time Lizzie sighed. "Time will tell. . . ."

chapter

9

Williams, Minnesota

BILLY LEFAVE DID not take the Canadian National train back
to Williams as he had planned. One of Meloney's teamsters,
Lars Jensen, had been heading west, saw Billy in Baudette,
and offered him a ride back.

"Be glad for the company, iffen you're wanting to hie
along."

"Don't mind if I do, Lars!" Billy said. "Thanks! I was ready
to head back anyway, and going with you will save me a
night's lodging and my train fare. I'll treat you to dinner at
the Grant Hotel when we get back."

"You don't have to do that!"

"I want to," Billy insisted.

"I'll enjoy Miss Lizzie's cooking, that's for sure!"

Lizzie wasn't expecting Billy's return that afternoon, for
the westbound train had already come and gone with no Billy
in sight and no other passengers either.

She couldn't help feeling a bit relieved, for nowadays the
hotel register was generally filled with paying customers and
they would've been crowded on space had there been new
arrivals in town.

The late-afternoon dinner hour was just beginning when
Billy and then Lars Jensen entered the dining room.

Lizzie rushed to greet Billy with a hug.

"What a surprise! Didn't expect you back so soon."

"I'm like a bad penny, I reckon, Ma. Here I am! And with a friend in tow. We're both hungry for a big plate of whatever you have plenty of," Billy said, then whispered, "Put Lars' meal on my tab. He gave me a ride back to town—saved me train fare."

"Nonsense!" Lizzie said. "I made plenty. His kindness to you was a kindness to us and will be repaid the same. Lots o' fresh vegetables from Brad's garden, so's it ain't like we're givin' away food charged to Rose Ames. Brad's been donatin' his produce to the coffers right along."

"Whatever," Billy said and gratefully took a seat, as did the lumberman.

"I'll bring you each a cup of coffee 'n cream," Lizzie said, not having to be informed that's what they needed. She could tell that Billy was tired and needed to relax over coffee, prepare for his meal, and get a chance to become rejuvenated.

Lizzie, sensitive, didn't inquire about how Billy's business had gone, because she suspected it was not good or he'd have burst into the hotel, elated, wonderful news and myriad details helplessly on his lips.

Instead he was strangely stoic.

"Wonderful meal, Miss Lizzie!" the lumber company employee said when he'd enjoyed a second after-dinner cup of coffee. "But I must be hurrying on."

"Thanks for seein' my boy home to me," Lizzie said. "Don't be a stranger to us, Lars. C'mon back!"

No sooner had the lumberman exited the dining room and given them privacy than Lizzie sank into the chair just vacated by Billy's dinner companion.

"Tell me, Son . . . how'd it go in Baudette?"

Billy sighed, wordlessly shook his head, then stared off, as if sightless, to the stonework fireplace in the adjoining lobby.

"Not very good. Not good at all."

"You look lower'n a snake's belly," Lizzie admitted.

"And feel even lower," Billy acknowledged.

"What happened?"

"For starters, the banker was one of those fancy-Dan city fellows who doesn't appear to have done a hard day's labor in his life. One of those bookish debit-and-credit blokes who only understands facts, figures, income, outgo, capital, and financial statistics."

"A feller with no imagination, mmmmm?" Lizzie mused.

"I guess you could say that. . . ."

"In other words, your current holdings, your physical health, your work ethic didn't count for much?"

"That's pretty much the long and short of it. And I didn't have any wealthy friends to sign as backers."

"He turned you down pretty flat, didn't he?"

"So fast that I almost caught pneumonia from the whirlwind he created!"

Lizzie couldn't help a wan chuckle at the picture.

"And the other feller at the second bank?"

"Same story."

"Oh, Will. I'm so sorry."

"I know, Ma. But not as sorry as me. I wish there was something I could do. I feel so helpless."

"And like most o' us, you don't like that feelin' a'tall."

"Reckon I don't."

"Can't blame you there. But don't you go forgettin', William LeFave, that we're never helpless and we're never alone, because greater is he whose Spirit lives within us than all o' the forces of the world. The Lord's got an answer in this."

"I'm not holding my breath waiting."

"Didn't suggest that you should! Sometimes these situations take time."

"Maybe it's not what I'm meant to do. But it felt so right. Maybe I counted on it too much. And now—"

"You're bitterly disappointed."

Billy nodded, not even speaking, and Lizzie wasn't sure that he wasn't going to end up wiping tears.

"When I think of all the money that I've made in my days—and squandered or lost—it makes me feel plumb ill! If only I had that cash now, when I would appreciate it and use it wisely instead of spendin' it like a carousing fool!"

"The past's the past, Will. You learned a hard lesson, I reckon, and paid cash tuition in the school of hard knocks. Sure as I'm sittin' here, I know that the Lord has a wonderful plan in store for you. Don't get weakhearted over this setback. So many times something seems tragical, and then, when life seems its bleakest—like the dark hour of the soul that Scripture talks about—there's a new dawn, and real joy comes with the morning."

" . . . I know," Billy said, nodding, but his conviction seemed shaken.

Lizzie arose to get them more coffee. She gave Billy's muscular shoulder a loving, consoling pat as she brushed by.

"You just trust in the Lord, Will. I've said more'n a time or two that when the Lord decides to move in a person's life, then ya'll had better grab your hat 'n hang on for the ride. Jesus Christ can open doors fast enough to create bigger whirlwinds than the banker in his turndown!"

Billy managed a weak smile.

Lizzie winked, grabbed the dress-up, prosperous hat that

Luke had lent to the cause, mashed it down on Billy's head, and said, "Hang on!"

He did, zealously so, and muttered, "I'm ready for my miracle!"

"You'll get it, William LeFave, and don't you doubt it for a moment! You goin' to remain in Williams for worship services the day after tomorrow?"

"I thought I would," Billy said.

"Good! Then the congregation can join hands and pray over the matter."

"I'll head out to the lake on Monday morning."

"That'll work out hunky-dory," Lizzie said, nodding. "Serenity's wantin' to spend a couple o' days with her people."

"Be glad to have her company. She's a sweet girl."

"I'm feelin' that they don't come any finer than Way-Say-Com-a-Gouk."

"If you don't mind, I'll pass that knowledge on to the chief."

"Go ahead. A parent can't hear too many favorable reports about a child. Give him my regards, too!"

"Consider it done!"

Lizzie had disappeared for fresh coffee and returned to take her seat when there were footsteps in the hallway. She glanced over her shoulder in time to see Lolly Ravachek hesitantly and sleepily move into the dining room, as if in a daze.

"Well, good morning!" Lizzie's hotel manager's personality took over.

"Good day," Lolly said, smiling, looking at Lizzie and then beyond to the handsome man.

Lizzie caught the flash of interest in the gypsy woman's eyes. She was used to the town's marriageable females casting such glances in her attractive son-in-law's direction.

"Hungry?" Lizzie inquired, knowing that Lolly should be, for she hadn't shown her face in several days.

"Yes."

"I'll get you a menu," Lizzie said. "Where would you like to sit, Miss?"

Billy, ever the gentleman and noting that the dining room was otherwise empty and that the woman would occupy a lonely table, said, "She could join us, Ma. She might enjoy companionship!"

"How thoughtless of me not to think of that!" Lizzie said blithely after she recovered, but she felt a sinking inside that Billy had suggested it.

There was something about the gypsy seer that put Lizzie's teeth on edge and kept them there. Ordinarily one who felt "the more the merrier," she'd not wanted her time with Billy in the hotel's dining room marred by another's presence— especially not that of Lolita Ravachek!

"Why . . . thank you!" Lolly said.

Instantly Billy was on his feet, edging the chair back so that he could assist her in a gentlemanly fashion.

Lizzie sighed, quailing inwardly. But Ma Preston had raised her right, and she swallowed hard and began introductions.

"Miss Lolita Ravachek, please meet my *son-in-law*, William LeFave!"

Lizzie felt inner satisfaction when she saw evidence that Lolly was disappointed to learn that Billy was an "in-law," and Lizzie didn't miss it when Lolly's eyes flicked to the ring finger, left hand, where the wedding band that Harmony had given her beloved still remained.

"Welcome to Williams, Miss Lolita," Billy said.

"Thank you, Mr. LeFave."

"Call me Billy or Will, even William," he said.

WILLIAM! Understanding jolted through Lolly like a thunderbolt. She almost laughed out loud and in delighted relief at the realization. Of course! The tarot cards and crystal ball had seemed to reveal "Williams," but the last letters had been hazy and indistinct.

At that moment, she knew that she truly had been meant to go to *Williams* to meet a man she would marry: *William!* The sometimes maliciously capricious spirits had no doubt enjoyed toying with her, savoring her confusion and consternation. It was one of their mysterious half-truths when she'd discovered the reprehensible human being awaiting her on the depot platform.

But it had needed to be like that!

The marriage-minded lumberjack had been used to bring her to Williams so she would soon meet the truly marriageable man for her.

"How nice to meet you," Lolly said, extending her hand.

"The pleasure is all mine," Billy said, accepting her grip.

Accustomed to receiving psychometric impressions and revelations from the spirit realm, Lolly held it a moment longer than necessary and might have continued a few seconds more except that Lizzie cleared her throat and moved between the pair to deposit a coffee cup in front of the gypsy woman.

"Thank you, ma'am," Lolly said absently, then seemed to dismiss Lizzie's presence as she turned back to the handsome Frenchman, her expression enthusiastic as her eyes remained oddly and eerily distant. "Do you have interest in this hotel, William?" Lolly asked to get the conversation going.

"Heavens no, although I do help out a spell! My late wife's ma and pa are managing it for the owners, who reside elsewhere."

"Late wife? Oh ... I'm so sorry to hear that," Lolly said,

realizing that it was expected of her. She'd already discovered that William LeFave was a widower, via their mere touch, which had also transmitted a myriad of other awarenesses.

Lizzie felt a strange, needling resentment prickle through her. The girl was a bare-faced liar! She wasn't sorry about Harmony's passing at all! If anything, Lolly was purely, unadulteratedly relieved that her competition for Billy was perfectly and permanently out of her manipulative way.

"What do you do for a living, William?"

Lizzie didn't trust Billy in the conversation. She took charge.

"He has lakeside property, a long, long, long ways from town. No neighbors 'ceptin' for Indians, and he makes his living fishing, trapping, 'n doing things, so he doesn't spend a lot of time at his property."

Billy stared at Lizzie. He'd never heard her use such words, and although he knew she had utmost respect for what he'd done with his life, at that moment, despite the fact he knew it couldn't possibly be true . . . he felt as if his trusted, revered, lovable mother-in-law were running him down!

"So you're a trapper?" Lolly trilled.

"A *poor* trapper," Billy found himself clarifying, wishing he could bite the derogatory, defeated words back even as they fell off his lips.

Lolly suddenly giggled. "You certainly are a humble man! Or have exceptionally high financial standards! For you have lots of money!" The exotically beautiful gypsy girl laid her hand on Billy's arm. "No doubt about it!" she affirmed at the almost jolting contact.

Billy and Lizzie cast quick glances at the gypsy girl.

Billy was the first to recover. "If that's true, then you must know something that the banker and I aren't aware of."

"Perhaps I do . . .," Lolly said.

"Oh . . . no . . .," Lizzie whispered, so faintly that only she was aware of the muted, miserable sound that escaped her.

Before Lizzie could react and come between her son-in-law and the suddenly vivacious gypsy girl who looked as if she hung on every word Billy spoke, Lolly took Billy's large hand in her small, soft, almost embracing grip.

"You're a rich man!" Lolly intoned. "Your fortune doth await your claiming it. . . ."

Billy gave a nervous laugh and glanced helplessly up at his mother-in-law, who stared in silent, expressionless horror.

"I see an island . . .," Lolly said, closing her eyes, continuing to cling to Billy's hand, and it was as if he hadn't the life, will, nor control to remove it from her tightening grip. "Very lonely. Remote. . . . There is a drunken man . . . oh! it's *you*, William . . . digging in the sand . . . making sure that you are not watched. . . ."

What's the matter with her? Billy mouthed toward Lizzie, but Lolly, whose eyes remained closed, did not see.

The thin-lined expression on Lizzie's face conveyed her sentiments without so much as the utterance of a syllable.

You don't want to know, Will! her eyes flashed the dismal message.

Billy shrank back, as if touched by something evil, and Lolly was almost pulled out of her chair in her desperate grip to hang on.

"The island! It's the place of much unhappiness. Killings! A long . . . long . . . time ago. Your gold is there. . . ."

Lolly seemed to drift out of a trance just as Lizzie, unable to bear it a moment longer, tore herself away from the disturbing scene and fled to the kitchen for a plate of food, in hopes that the gypsy girl would gobble it down and be on her way, out the door, and onto the first train leaving Williams!

When Lizzie returned, Lolly was no longer in a trance state, but Lizzie noticed that Billy was so preoccupied and distant that it was almost as if he were.

Lizzie thought Lolly would never excuse herself and return to her quarters.

Finally it happened.

"Will, come in the kitchen with me right now!" Lizzie said in such a no-nonsense tone that it brooked no argument. Billy arose and almost reluctantly followed her into the kitchen, as if he expected, startlingly enough, that he was going to catch the dickens from his mother-in-law—and he had no idea over *what*.

"You're upset!" Billy quietly observed.

"You'd better believe I am—and you should be, too! Don't you believe a word of what she said to you, William LeFave. That fortune-teller claptrap is all ungodly hogwash. Ain't a shred o' truth in it! So don't you go fritterin' away your time chasin' after some pot o' gold at the end of the rainbow and wear yourself out diggin' around on islands. You just stick to the straight and narrow, work hard, and your day will come! This is just a deception to trick you into wastin' time."

" . . . How did she know, Ma?" Billy asked, his voice quiet and confused.

"Know what? . . .," Lizzie gulped.

"What she knew, Ma—it's true. All of it. I was too drunk to recollect it myself, until she provided the words to prime my own memories. I did bury a lot of gold one time, gold earned from trapping, hiring out to guide others, 'n such honest labors. And it was on an island. I did check around a lot to make sure I wasn't watched. And there were a lot of murders committed on the island that I chose . . . which is why I chose it—it had an eerie and very unsavory history. I knew that lots of folks feared it for that reason alone, wouldn't go near it, so my fortune was safe to await my return...."

"Will, no!" an anguished Lizzie cried.

"Back in the 1700s, when Pierre LaVerendrye and his sons and nephew and a group of voyageurs from Montreal explored this area, along with the company was a young, devout man of God who came to the area, a missionary who desired to bring Christ to the savages. The pastor and his company of over a dozen people were massacred by the Sioux. Other Indians, aware that a man they considered allied with the Great Spirit had been killed, grew fearful of that island ever after."

"Then . . . there . . . is such a . . . place?"

Billy nodded. "White men now call it Massacre Island, for the slaughter of martyrs that took place there. It's up there in Canadian waters, not too far—considering the vastness of the Lake of the Woods—from the Northwest Angle, the nation's farthest point to the north. . . . The Indians know it as Devil's Island . . . and they give it wide berth, being fearful of the evil spirits that they believe dwell there now."

"Oh Will, this is horrible! Worse than I'd imagined—"

"How can it be horrible, Ma?! I'll get my hard-earned money that I'd considered lost for good and had released unto the Lord, accepting his will that I not recall where 'twas buried, fearing that perhaps money might be the ruination of me as a man. At one time, it would've been, but now . . . I'm changed . . . and how wisely I'll finance my dreams, seeing stewardship entrusted to me with the wealth—and the bankers be switched!"

" . . . That's true enough. But . . ."

"Maybe it's that miracle you were talking about, Ma. You

told me to grab my hat and hang on for the ride." He stroked Luke's hat, which he would soon return to him. "If there's as much gold there as I remember burying . . . there'll be no more borrowed hats for me! And our little church is going to have a brand-new bell, hymnals, and so many other things with my tithe!"

Lizzie felt truly torn.

"Fortune-tellers and the like, Will, they're evil people. A person shouldn't have truck with them."

"I didn't seek her out," Billy said. "She just appeared. I'm confused about this, too, Ma. I'd never consult her on purpose, that's for sure. She just supplied what seems like a miracle."

"I know. God does work in mysterious ways," Lizzie mused, her brow furrowed as she tried to figure it all out.

"My own life's proof enough that the Lord can use everything—good or bad—to eventually serve his purposes."

" . . . I . . . know. . . . I'll admit that, Will, but I'm plumb nervous about the woman. Don't know what to think about her. My instincts ain't good on the matter. . . . Brad, he knows how I feel, and he warrants that we should just continue our Christian walk through life and at least consider that perhaps the Lord's sent such a strange and disturbing woman into our midst because it's his plan to save her to himself 'n deliver her from her present involvements."

"Could be," Billy said. "Two years ago I wasn't what anyone would've considered a likely candidate to become a committed Christian, either. And look what happened to me! All because good Christian people loved this poor sinner, even as they hated his dark and ugly sins."

"Reckon you and Brad are right and that she deserves the same. Iffen the Lord—"

"We could always invite her to Sunday worship services," Billy suggested.

"S'pose we could," Lizzie agreed. Then she quickly added, "Ya leave that invitation to me, you hear?!" Lolly had quite enough high-minded ambitions regarding William LeFave, Lizzie feared, without his innocent, compassionate actions spawning more deviousness and devilment on Lolly's part.

Billy looked startled at how flinty Lizzie was on the subject.

"Sure, Ma," he quickly agreed.

"I'll attend to it," Lizzie promised, "and see what she says."

She withheld the knowledge that she felt she had to do it herself so that Lolly Ravachek would feel free to accept or reject the idea of her own free will and not instinctively decide to go along just because it offered her a chance to be near Billy LeFave.

Lizzie sensed—knew—that if the handsome, widowed William LeFave were to ask the attractive . . . witch . . . to worship services, there'd be no choice in the matter. Wild horses wouldn't keep Lolly away!

Lizzie felt no enthusiasm about inviting Lolly Ravachek to accompany them to church services Sunday morning, but she felt obligated to do so and did.

She'd wondered if she'd be able to do so, for she saw little of Lolly that evening and the following day.

Brad was present when the opportunity arose.

Lizzie broached the topic.

And Brad stepped in and echoed the invitation convincingly.

"It'll give you a chance to meet the folks in this town, Miss Lolly. You're more'n welcome to go along! Most everyone'll be there. Hotel staff, Lemont, Bill, Serenity, the Mastersons, Wellinghams, Lundstens, Meloneys, Bonneys, Gillies, and other townspeople. . . ."

Lizzie sensed that the only name in the litany that meant a whit to Lolly Ravachek was Bill's.

"I'd like to, but—"

"But what?" Brad said.

" . . . I've never been to church services before. I—I don't know if I'll know what to do. I wouldn't want to make a fool of myself—or embarrass you people after you've been so wonderful about making me feel welcome. Even inviting me to attend church with you."

"Just do what everyone else does," Lizzie said. "Ain't no one goin' to judge you iffen you don't know the words. Be glad to see you, they will! Heavens, there was a time when none o' us had been inside a church, either, although for most of us, we attended the first time as babes in arm."

Lolly drew a deep breath, almost as if for courage, and said, "I'll be there! Thanks for inviting me."

"Don't worry about a way there, Miss Lolly," Brad said. "Guests of the hotel just ride along wit' fam'bly. Generally sit with us, too."

That Sunday morning, there were so many guests and family members that Brad had to make two trips to get everyone to church in the horse-drawn wagon.

By the time Lizzie entered the church with Brad, others were seated. Instantly Lizzie noticed that Lolly Ravachek was seated at Billy's right. Then, almost with relief, she saw that Serenity was seated at his left. The two women were positioned like beautiful bookends.

Attending church services was totally foreign to Lolly, but her ability to know things at a touch remained with her. When Serenity, the Chippewa girl, had been given a hand up into the conveyance by Mr. LeFave, Lolly had reached out to give her assistance.

At the touch of Serenity's hand in her own grip, Lolly knew—and almost gasped at what had been revealed to her!

The Indian girl had caused the death of Billy LeFave's beloved—in a roundabout way, to be sure, but any way one sliced it, Serenity was to blame. Lolly was aware that Billy did not even know that. Nor was Billy cognizant of the fact that Serenity loved and wanted him very much, something Serenity apparently kept well hidden from everyone but was unable to secret away from Lolly's piercing knowledges.

Knowing that Serenity liked her no better than she did the serene-eyed Indian maiden, Lolly made a graceful point of managing to sit next to William, as Serenity did on the other side, and Lolly knew a mean delight in realizing that she'd ruined the Sunday morning services for Serenity due to her proximity.

Lolly had not expected that she would feel any effect of attending church services one way or the other. She was startled to find within herself strange, strong, and swirling reactions. She chewed down on her lip—hard—to contain the emotions that bubbled within her like vicious brew in a witch's cauldron, threatening to spew forth uncontainably to shock and scandalize the prim and proper townspeople in attendance.

Vicious and vile oaths and obscenities seemed to scream in Lolly's mind until the pastor's words were all but drowned out by the powerful force. Lolly's head throbbed. She wished she could cup her aching temples and ease the agonizing pain, but it was as if her body were numb, and she was powerless to do anything.

A tickle in Lolly's throat caused her to cough without effect or relief, creating what she sensed was an irritation for the people who strained ahead to better hear the preacher. When they seemed to surge closer as they changed positions, she felt as if she were being buried alive. Lolly felt as though she were breaking out in a cold sweat, as if her very inner body were sinking away from itself, and for long, horrible moments she was afraid that she was going to embarrass herself and retch in front of the entire congregation.

By the time services ended, even though Lolly had not taken part and had sat through services as if she'd been stunned by a well-aimed blow between the eyes from a poleax, Lizzie was feeling better about the whole situation, if only from the power of the Word and the encouragement and edification of other believers strong in their reliance upon the Lord.

But her spirits plummeted when they filed out after the closing benediction.

There was a smile on Serenity's face. But when her eyes met Lizzie, a flash of understanding passed between them, and Lizzie—and only Lizzie—saw the pure, unadulterated misery that emanated from eyes that had so recently revealed great joy.

Lizzie knew that Lolly Ravachek had romantic designs on Billy LeFave . . . and Serenity was aware of it, too.

And Serenity liked that fact no better than she!

Lizzie was helpless not to be grateful that Billy and Serenity were leaving for the lakeside in the morning.

Perhaps by the time they returned to Williams, Lolly Ravachek would be long gone. . . .

chapter
10

Williams, Minnesota

BY THE TIME Billy LeFave returned Serenity to Williams after
a week's vacation with the tribe, Lolly Ravachek had not
departed as Lizzie had previously hoped. Also, Lizzie had suffered moments of inexplicable animosity toward the girl—
emotions that she was helpless to contain—to the point
where both Lester and Brad had confronted her about it,
wondering what was the matter.

"She just gives me the crawlies, that's all!" Lizzie defend-
ed, her face flushed from the sting of criticism. "I can't help
how I feel!"

"You can't help how you feel," Brad agreed. "But the Lord
can help you with those feelings. Maybe you don't like the girl
very well—but don't forget that he loves her as he loves all o'
us. Enough to die for her sins, too, payin' her debt iffen she'll
humble herself to accept his sacrifice and restitution for her
own sins, just as he settled the accounts for all of us 'cause we
were too spiritually bankrupt to begin to do anythin' about it."

"I know. I have been trying," Lizzie said.

"I'm aware of that. And it's my estimation that Lolly seems
to really be warmin' to you, honey. You have a way with
people, 'specially young and lonely girls without a mama of
their own to counsel and comfort them."

"I'd thought as much myself at times. But there's still something about her that really bothers me!"

"She's goin' to church regular. Takin' part. And in my way of lookin' at it—seems to be thirstin' for knowledge about the Word. Unless I'm seein' what I want to see instead of what's actually reality."

"Only the Lord knows," Lizzie said.

Lolly's church attendance—after the first time, when she'd seemed so strangely ill that no one had expected her to return, as she ended up doing—was a fact with which Lizzie could not argue. There were moments when Lizzie wondered if she was being unreasonable, if she was feeling petty because Harmony's husband was so obviously the focus of Lolly's attentions. Would she have felt bristly toward anyone who showed an interest in Billy—aside from Serenity, whom Lizzie was aware grieved for Harmony as much as she did or more?

"Y'know, you're a right smart woman, Liz," Brad began, his words careful. "But sometimes all o' us can benefit from another's wisdom. I'll admit—I don't know what to tell you about the situation. That's how Les feels, too. It was his idea that I propose to you that iffen these doubts and crawly feelin's continue to plague you . . . whyn't you seek out Pastor Edgerton and discuss the matter with him? He's an educated man of the cloth, knowledgeable in the Good Book, seminary trained. Surely he'd know how to guide us in this."

Lizzie's mouth gaped. Impulsively she hugged her husband hard.

"Brad, that's an absolutely wonderful idea! I'm goin' to do just that! Can you believe me, Brad Mathews? The way I've suggested to folks that they take their heavy troubles to their preacher—and I have to be reminded of it myself. Why didn't I think of that on my own?"

"Reckon that maybe you weren't meant to."

Or maybe I was blinded to it, a frightened part of Lizzie quietly wondered, *by a spirit of confusing delusion.* . . .

There were days when Lizzie now felt as if she hardly knew herself. And she certainly didn't know where the unusual thoughts, perceptions, and ideas came from. They were so unfamiliar that they didn't feel a part of her—and if they were of her, then there were areas of herself that she didn't like a'tall!

Lizzie frowned as she thought back.

And it had all begun to occur at the same time that Lolly Ravachek came to town.

Was Lolly in Williams that she could be led to the Lord by the loving Christians in the close-knit community, who'd show her Christian love while hating the evil acts she'd done?

Or was she a very attractive, well-mannered, unsuspected emissary from hell, guided by dark spirits whose only desire was to spiritually contaminate Christians? Would she tear down that which faith in the Lord had wrought in the wilderness pioneer town? Would she destroy that which thrived in the white clapboard house of God? There Lolly Ravachek was welcomed cordially enough, even as Lizzie—and perhaps some others—privately suspected she was an interloper hellbent on their destruction.

Come the next Monday morning, Lizzie Mathews, wearing her Sunday best, leaving Joy and Serenity in charge of the hotel dining room, walked to the parsonage.

The pastor's wife, Lydia, with their three-year-old son, Levi, in tow, met her at the door.

"What a surprise!" Lydia Edgerton cried, giving her friend an embrace as Lizzie rumpled Levi's silky brown hair. "How good to see you!"

After exchanging pleasantries with Lydia and Levi, Lizzie got down to business.

"I'm afraid I'm here to consult with the pastor over a difficult problem, more than as the purely social call that I'd rather it could be. Is the pastor in . . . so I can make an appointment to speak with him? . . ."

Before Lydia Edgerton could reply, her husband entered the room, with his hand outstretched.

"He sure is!" Pastor Edgerton said. "And if you've got the time now, Lizzie, I'll take the time."

"You're sure it's not an imposition?"

"Positive. Come in!"

"Levi and I have some tasks in the garden," Lydia said, "so if you'll excuse us . . ."

"Of course," Lizzie said, grateful that the pastor's wife had graciously extended them privacy for the conversation.

Lizzie was relieved over that. After all, with her basic sense of decency long-instilled, whatever her personal feelings might be, she desired to give the raven-haired, exotically beautiful gypsy girl the benefit of the doubt. She certainly didn't wish to risk alienating others in the congregation from the newcomer, creating biases in them based on what she'd learned.

After leading Lizzie into his study, the pastor suggested, "Let's pray before we begin."

"I'd love that," she agreed.

They bowed their heads, and he prayed, "Lord, according to the Word, you promise that wherever two or more are gathered in your name, you are present. We are trusting that you will be with us to guide us in wisdom and strength, extending special grace to us as we seek to solve a problem and do it according to your will, that it be pleasing in your sight. . . ."

A moment later the pastor cleared his throat, got comfortable in the chair behind his desk while Lizzie was seated in a cozy occasional chair.

"What can I help you with, Lizzie?"

Nervously Lizzie licked her lip. Words seemed to swirl wildly in her mind—frustratingly so—with the result that she didn't know where to even begin.

"Well, there's this problem, Reverend," she began, trying to collect and organize her chaotic thoughts. "At least, I think there's a problem."

The pastor steepled his fingers together and solemnly regarded the middle-aged believer.

"You're a no-nonsense woman, Lizzie, not given to flights of fantasy nor groundless concerns. You're well versed in the Word and integrate it into your daily walk. If you feel there's a problem of some sort, then most likely there is, and I'd like to help you. That's what I'm here for."

"It's like this," Lizzie began, drawing a deep breath. "This's been heavy on my heart and mind for a few weeks now. It's been that way ever since I laid eyes on this individual. I've tried to conquer my feelin's, asked the Lord to help me, and that's worked some . . . but there's *somethin'*, and I cain't even quite discern *what*, but it's disturbin' me terribly. . . ."

"I'll ask in confidence, and you can reply in the same, knowing that your words will go no farther. Who's troubling you?"

" . . . Lolly Ravachek. . . ."

"What's the matter?"

"I don't rightly know—but I've sure got my ideas!"

"And? . . ."

"There's somethin' really radical wrong with her. I—I'm purty convinced that she's a *witch* . . . or *something* awful like that!"

Lizzie's words fell flat, the accusation ugly even to her own ears. Before the pastor could react and respond and brush away her concerns with the suggestion that perhaps she was overreacting to something, Lizzie rushed on with a jumble of evidentiary behaviors, observations, and a chronicling of events in the hotel, including Lolly's strange, otherworldly power to inform Billy LeFave of where he'd buried a cache of gold coins some years earlier.

The pastor's expression grew more thoughtful, then edged toward becoming an alarmed frown. Several times, Lizzie apologized for rambling and rattling so much, not giving him a chance to speak, but he simply gestured for her to go on in her explanations. Finally she felt she was through. Sharing her concerns with the pastor had made the burden feel lighter already.

"Do you know anything about such things?" Lizzie asked. "About fortune-tellers, witchcraft, whatever it is?"

The pastor gave a weary sigh, seeming suddenly old for one whom Lizzie had considered to be youthfully in his prime.

"Unfortunately—or perhaps it is actually fortunate—but yes. Yes, I do. I've had little practical experience myself, but we studied such areas in our seminary training. One of our professors of theology, a grand old gentleman, taught us far more than was mentioned between the pages of textbooks."

"Thank the Lord!" Lizzie breathed.

"He had vast experiences in that realm, experiences that accumulated during his years as a missionary on the Dark Continent."

"Africa?"

"Yes. He told truly horrendous testimonies. His personally and others he'd been aware of as well. Situations like something from the pen of the late Edgar Allan Poe—and worse!"

"Heavens!" Lizzie murmured, her eyes widening.

"Thank goodness you don't think I'm demented, comin' to you like this."

"Not at all. Scripture warns us that evil forces will attack us and that we're dealing with powers and principalities. Dark and evil forces in the world will use anyone or anything to try to oppress others—most especially Christians. And we're warned that the Devil himself will disguise himself as an angel of light in his desire to fool and subvert God's children. Alas, sometimes the individuals most lethal to our spiritual lives, we find ourselves fond of in the human realm."

"That's what it's like for me! I feel plumb torn—wantin' to find cause to like Lolly on one hand, but on t'other feelin' like she's anathema, with me left wishin' I'd never met her. Wonderin' one day iffen the Lord's sent her in our direction 'cause he wants us to guide and edify her and help her to know him as her Savior, or"—she was helpless not to give a shudder—"suspectin' she's someone that we're bein' . . . fooled . . . into likin' and acceptin' . . . and it's a dark and evil plan to wean us away from the purity of the Word, cause divisions 'n suspicions among believers, or in many other ways, result in works of devilment within a Christian community."

"We'll not know until the Lord reveals his purpose to us. We need discernment. And the will to do his will, so that we are there for Lolly if he intends for her to one day be his own. And yet be strong in him, girded in all the defenses of faith, if this is but a crafty, diabolical attack using a very pretty and congenial . . . weapon. . . ."

"It could be either—couldn't it?" Lizzie murmured, realizing that she'd hoped that the pastor could give her a clearcut answer but knowing that was unrealistic.

He nodded. "These things take time and call for much prayer, even fasting. I've noticed in my calling and when I was in the seminary that it seems when the power of the Lord is strong in a church . . . so often that's when satanic forces begin to move, doing what they can to detour those who'd spread the Gospel to the hurting, needy, lost souls who were born captive into Satan's kingdom and can only be liberated by accepting the blood of Christ on the cross and being born anew as spiritual sons and daughters in the kingdom of God.

"Doubtless you're as familiar with the concepts as I," Pastor Edgerton said, then briefly outlined the fall of man, and human beings' need for redemption, and the end result, which was that there was warfare on earth and in heaven. The battle for souls still raged, he said, even though Satan had been defeated at the cross over nineteen hundred years before with Jesus' death.

"Sometimes I wonder why the Good Lord didn't slap Satan down good and proper, throw him into the fiery lake, 'n be done with it all long ago!" Lizzie blurted.

The pastor only chuckled. "Our God is just and fair, Lizzie, slow to anger and great in mercy. The Lord is honest and dependable. We can trust him, because he's never whimsical. The universe was created with a mysterious brilliance beyond human understanding, imbued with natural laws and order in the universe. The Lord, who created these natural laws, does not change them for his own convenience. Therefore two parts of hydrogen and one part of oxygen *always* results in water. Be it ice, snow, or rain. You see, we'd have a hard time trusting a Creator who'd made a world so that one time such a combination of elements made water, and another time it came out tomato juice, or sand, or a pansy."

"That's true enough," Lizzie agreed, having a sudden appreciation that when she planted a kernel of corn, she knew what to expect come harvest.

"The Lord God keeps his word with all. He does not go

back on his covenants . . . even though men break them. God is just and honest—even when he is dealing with a lying, cheating, betraying deceiver like Satan. . . ."

"Like it says in the Book of Job?"

"Exactly! Satan—who was called Lucifer and was the Light Bearer until his pride caused him to be cast from heaven— was created with great knowledge and power and was in a very high position. But not high enough to suit him . . . for he wanted to be worshiped above the God who created him. There's a battle for souls. When Adam and Eve sinned, all was lost to Satan. But God had a plan of redemption through Jesus Christ. Satan, in his prideful jealousy, counterfeits what's true in the kingdom of God, and creates fraudulently comparable abilities in the dark realm."

"I don't doubt you," Lizzie said, frowning, "but I don't really catch what you're drivin' at."

"There are gifts of the Spirit," the pastor said, "God-given abilities instilled within believers."

Lizzie nodded. "Yes. . . ."

"Satan duplicates these abilities with counterfeits. A believer in unity with the Holy Spirit may possess a gift of knowledge. A human being in league with dark forces, knowingly or unwittingly, may become a gifted and accurate fortuneteller. It's Satan's way of luring curious and impatient people into consulting dark spirits rather than trusting in the Lord."

"And most times, folks ain't even aware of who . . . or what . . . is behind the ungodly predictions, is that it? So they assume it's of God?"

"Right you are, Lizzie. No doubt you've heard it said many times, as have I, that the Devil is at his strongest when people scoff and doubt that he really even exists."

"And the Good Lord gets blamed for a lot o' stuff he didn't do—'n didn't sanction."

The pastor nodded. "Simply *allowed* Satan to get away with, because the Lord is fair, just, and righteous. Like in the Book of Job . . . when he gave the Devil permission to test Job. It's all a matter of will. God's will. Our free will. The Lord's plan and purpose for us. Satan's attempts to keep us from fulfilling that. And then the Lord's ultimate will, which can never be defeated."

Lizzie knew she had solid grounding in Scripture, had been educated and edified at almost countless worship services and revivals over the years, but she sensed her knowledge was not as complete as it could be.

"I'm not sure I really understand," she admitted.

"There's frequently some confusion when we talk about the will of God, for it's like there are several layers of meaning to be understood and merged together for clarity.

"There's God's intentional will. That's what he would have us do for perfection in our lives. That's no guarantee we'll do what he intends . . . because we're free not to.

"Then there's the permissive will of God. In our fallen world, we deal with that situation frequently. Jesus told us that the Father would have that none would perish. That's his intentional will for us. But reality is that we can choose to do terrible things to one another—and while God permits this and allows it to happen, that does not mean that it is his will for us. For it isn't. It is his permissive will, and he knows that we will learn from it, become strengthened, and one day it will end up contributing to his ultimate will . . . when, in the end, everything—good and bad—has resulted in fulfilling the perfect plan and purpose for mankind as conceived by God. You may remember, Lizzie, that I touched on similar concepts when you were so broken by Harmony's death ... and Thad's. ..."

Lizzie nodded. "I reckon I was too addlepated and wretched at the time to have it stick 'n make sense," she said in a rueful tone. "But it's stickin' now!"

"Great!"

"I feel better, layin' all o' this out to you for your insights 'n wisdom. Even if it don't really give me any more clear-cut way in how I'm to deal with Lolly."

"We're called to love the sinner as we hate the sin. As Christians, we can extend love and charity to her—and withhold any condemnation—until it would become apparent that criticism is in order. And then something can—and will—be done about it."

" ... Like 'the testimony of two men'?"

"Exactly. I pray that it won't come to that," the pastor said. "But if she should desire to practice her dark arts in this town ... the people of God will confront her and point out the error of her ways."

"And do it in a spirit o' love 'n carin'," Lizzie mused.

"I should hope so," the pastor murmured. "After all, being born with a sinful nature and being heirs to Satan's dark kingdom, many goodhearted and likable people have no idea of the abominations they perform. If they're lovingly informed of their errors instead of angrily accused, great wonders can be wrought in turning them away from Satan's blinding confusion and freeing them with the light of Christ's truth."

"We can pray that it happens," Lizzie said, arising, feeling as if the weight of the world had been removed from her, with her problem—the town's concerns—so willingly shouldered by the intelligent, strong young pastor of solid faith.

"Not only for Lolly but for the entire town. We've a strong

Christian community," the pastor said. "But there are twice as many outside it as within. We've much work to do. So we can expect great resistance from dark forces, as in our zealously carrying the Gospel to unbelievers, we're a threat to Satan's stronghold. But knowing ahead that we are already victorious in Christ and protected by his precious blood and invested with believers' authority to command evil spirits in his name gives us power and assurance so that we need not fear."

"What a blessin' you are to this town, Pastor Edgerton! 'Twas a miracle in the makin' when Luke arranged for you to come to this region."

"I like to believe so," he said, smiling.

"I feel ever so much better now! Ready, willin', and prepared to face whatever I'm called on to deal with."

"That's good to hear, Lizzie. I'm grateful that we're serving on the same side in this battle."

"And servin' the same commander in chief," Lizzie pointed out, "Jesus Christ."

Promising Lydia that she'd return someday for tea and a purely social visit, Lizzie returned to the hotel—unaware that all the way she'd been humming "Onward Christian Soldiers."

Without Lizzie at the hotel, and with the new, strange woman present, Serenity was highly uncomfortable. She would have dogged Joy, as if seeking her companionship and protection, but they each had a specialized list of tasks to do that often required them to be in differing areas of the large hotel.

To Serenity it was as if the more pains she took to unobtrusively avoid Lolly Ravachek, the more regularly the gypsy woman popped up—almost like a perverse jack-in-the-box—to startle and alarm her with her presence. Serenity thought it was uncanny, and her gloom deepened with the unpleasant knowledge.

Although Serenity was becoming more fluent in her English, she purposely led Lolly to believe that her command of the language was almost nonexistent, so that the dark-haired beauty would leave her alone.

"Don't try to fool me, you murderer!" Lolly hissed when she finally got Serenity alone.

The Indian girl's dark eyes widened with alarm. "I know what you did," Lolly said, her voice arched with a sneer of triumph. "I know your deepest and darkest secrets!"

Serenity said nothing.

"You the same as murdered your best friend, taking that sick baby to her when you knew you weren't supposed to, when William had forbidden it."

Serenity felt her knees wobble and grow weak with dread and fright.

"You thought no one would ever know—but *I* know."

"So, so sorry . . .," Serenity whispered, and tears sprang to her eyes.

"I also know that you love William LeFave," Lolly said, and her voice dropped to a harsh hiss. "He's not for you—he's destined to be *mine!* And I'm going to see to it that I get what's due me! Stay away from William LeFave! Do you hear me?"

"No!" Serenity protested, her voice feeble with tears.

"*Yes!*" Lolly snapped the command. "You're going to stay away from him—or else. If you don't, I'm going to tell William what I know about what happened to his wife—all because of you! I'm aware that he has great fondness for you! But do you think that it'll last when he realizes that he's lost the love of his life because of *you*? Are you such a fool that you believe he can love the same woman who cost him his wife?"

"Please don't—no!" Serenity begged.

"Beware: stay away from William LeFave, or I'll tell him what I know about your past." For good measure, Lolly threw out a few facts that only Serenity could know, so she would conclude that because Lolly, a stranger to the area, knew them, she must possess strange and dangerous powers.

"Please, I beg in name of God! Don't!"

"Then, do as I say! Stay away from William—and discourage him so that he stays away from you!. . ."

chapter

11

Williams, Minnesota

WAR WAS WHAT Lizzie Mathews felt had been declared.

Not only within the premises of the Grant Hotel but without as well.

Her insights sharpened by the pastor's words of wisdom, she felt that she recognized more clearly what was going on, and she suspected the kind of forces that were at work.

There was an unpleasant, almost unidentified tension that seemed to weave itself around those who resided in the hotel, tangling them together, pulling in opposite directions, until many days ended not in a serene manner as before but in what Lizzie was helpless not to think of, speak about to Brad, in terms of "an evil, snarly mess!"

"How can it be?!" she cried. "Lolly's only one person. We outnumber her time 'n time again. How can she be such a bad influence on us—and we seem to have no effect on her?"

Brad shrugged. "It only takes a bit of yeast to leaven the loaf, darlin'. Remember that."

"What're we goin' to do?"

"Pray. And then pray some more. And realize that the Lord's will is bein' somehow served in all of this."

Lizzie had a difficult time reconciling that wisdom with what began to happen in the world around her.

Lolly, who seemed to be a woman of independent means, came and went as she saw fit, and she dared to go places—like to the Black Diamond Saloon—where no decent woman would've cast a shadow across the entrance. Not only did Lolly occasionally go to the tavern—worse, she seemed at home there, and the lumberjacks adored her.

Rumor had it that Lolly had been busy deflecting proposals of matrimony, to the point where she abandoned the saloon for the security of the Grant Hotel.

Even with the beautiful gypsy out of sight, she filled the minds of the rough and rowdy lumberjacks, and more than a few fights broke out between the men as they wrestled with jealous frustrations regarding the pretty, if unreachable, stranger.

And the saloon girls—who kept to themselves, seemed content with their lurid lot, and appreciated their place in the world, far removed from the town's chaste and Christian womenfolk—disliked Lolly intensely, for in her they found competition that they'd have preferred not to deal with. When allowed, she could play poker with the best of men, winning hand after hand until she was invited out of the game. After that, she could always guide a gent willing to share the pot with advice to bring him a winning hand.

Word soon spread. Lolly Ravachek was not only a beautiful and sprightly woman but there was something unusual about her. By various strange means, Lolly *knew* things that other folks simply didn't.

Williams was divided.

There were those who feared her and her ways.

And those who admired and adored her for her unusual abilities.

As the factions developed, within the hotel and without, Lizzie lived with a horrible sense of dread that something terrible was about to happen. In her heart . . . she knew that it was destined to take place . . . but she didn't know when.

She didn't know if the momentous occasion would herald a blessing.

Or if it would be like a special delivery from hell.

Only time would tell.

And with each passing moment, Lizzie seemed to feel herself grow more tense as she and those who joined in prayer with her and Pastor Edgerton awaited the coming moment of truth.

It was past dusk when Pastor Edgerton came to the Grant Hotel. His face was uncharacteristically grim. Lizzie's heart leaped to her throat. She realized that the moment she'd sensed was destined had arrived.

"Hello, Brad, Lizzie. . . . Could I have a word with you both? In private?" Pastor Edgerton asked.

"Of course," Brad said, gesturing toward the nearby business office.

He held the door open for the preacher. Lizzie whisked off her apron, tossed it at a hook on the kitchen wall, and was only a step or two behind the men.

"The moment we've all been praying about seems at hand," Pastor Edgerton said. "It's time for us to take action to defeat the errors of dark happenings."

"What's goin' on now?" Brad asked.

"Sven Larsen came to see me this evening. Lolly's been telling fortunes at the saloon. Earning money—as well as quite a reputation, I'm afraid. She knows so many hidden secrets about these men's pasts that they're trusting her about the future as if she were a prophet of God."

"Nothin' could be farther from the truth!"

"We know that," the pastor quietly said. "But she needs to be so informed. She seems like an intelligent and at times very pleasant young woman, if cruelly duped by demons. Very likely she has no idea of the . . . wickedness . . . of her ways.

She's to be pitied," the pastor said. "In her own way, I think she believes in a Creator, and she feels that these unusual abilities she has are a God-given talent. Many people involved in the occult feel that way, because they have not been told differently—nor had Scriptures pointed out showing the abominable error of their ways."

"You're going to confront her?" Brad said.

"I think the time has come. I'd like for strong Christian men, grounded in the Word and solid in faith, to join me in prayer before we approach her as a unified group."

" . . . Do you expect trouble?" Lizzie was helpless not to ask.

The pastor was thoughtful. "Trouble? Of course. Perhaps not from Lolly herself. But as we move against dark, invasive forces . . . we can be sure that there'll be a price we pay for standing strong in the Lord and striving to protect and preserve from harm what is his . . . while rescuing a captive from the dark kingdom."

"Count me in iffen you want me," Brad said.

"I was trusting you'd volunteer. What about Lester?"

"I'm sure my son would be honored to be called into such service by you, Reverend."

"What about Lem Gartner? Do you feel that he's up to—"

"He's agin', he is, but he's tough as a hank o' rawhide," Lizzie said.

"Liz has known Lemont years longer than I have," Brad said, "but that's my assessment of him, too. He's salt of the earth."

"Sven's a relatively new Christian," the pastor said. "But he's as strong in spirit as he is in body. If you think he's worthy, too, Brad, I'd like him a part of this."

"I'd have suggested him myself. Kind o' wish that Billy LeFave was in town, so he could be with us, too."

"But he's not. So he isn't meant to be involved in this.

Regardless, men like Sven and Billy who've walked the dark side themselves can offer valuable testimony in confrontations such as this. And they seem to be able to discern the spirits—for they met them in their old life and are familiar with their lies, deceits, and tempting suggestions."

"What about Luke? Or Marc?"

"Both good men," the pastor said. "I'd considered them. Luke's family, and so is Marc. But I don't want Lolly to see so many consanguine and matrimonial relatives that she thinks this is some kind of vendetta by your family."

"A point well taken," Brad said.

"I hadn't even considered that!" Lizzie admitted.

"Marc's so busy doing the Lord's work with his healing folks' bodies that I hesitate to put a further burden on him by asking him to become involved in this, if there's another to serve. I've been praying about it."

"The Lord will guide us," Brad said.

"Sven's out talking to several other men from the congregation," the pastor said. "We've tentative plans to meet at the parsonage for prayer." He sighed and his voice became grim but firm in faith. "And we'll go from there."

"God bless y'all," Lizzie murmured. "You can count on me to help give you prayer cover."

"That's what my Lydia offered, too. She's dressing Levi and putting a few items in a satchel. I trusted that she could come and spend the evening—maybe the night—at the hotel? That way we can use the parsonage for . . . the confrontation . . . if Miss Lolly is willing to meet with us."

"We can't force her," Brad agreed.

"What the girl's got ahead of her's got to be done from her own . . . free . . . will. . . ." Pastor Edgerton spoke the words with weighty solemnity. "There may be resistance. . . ."

"The Lord's in control," Brad reminded them all. "Ain't

nothin' goin' to happen 'ceptin' he allows it. As long as we're prayin', seekin' his will 'n prepared to do it, taking cover and refuge in his work on the cross, we've nothin' to fear. Greater is he within us . . . than the one within Lolly and those like her. . . ."

"My feelings exactly," the pastor said.

There were quiet but careful preparations going on at the Grant Hotel. Casual observers would've sensed that there was something afoot, because of the whispers of the hotel staff, but would not have suspected a grim and desperate confrontation between the forces of good and evil.

Lizzie was hugging Brad and Lester and giving them each a good-bye kiss and a few tender words of shared faith when Lydia Edgerton and Levi arrived. Not long after that, other men from the church began dropping by with their wives and young'uns so that the children could play together or take naps on the comfortable, plush lobby furniture while the womenfolk prayed and encouraged and edified one another through the long, dark hours of the night.

"Girls, we're accustomed to spendin' time with one another, enjoying pleasant pursuits," Lizzie began. "Tonight we're here in faithful earnest to help our menfolk do the Lord's work while we offer them a prayer cover to edify 'em in the coming dark and torturous moments they'll face, but with our knowledge that Satan has already been defeated and that the power of Christ, which it's our authority to use, can work miracles with those shackled by dark forces and demons. . . ."

"Amen," the pastor's wife fervently murmured.

"The Lord loves our praise 'n our gratitude, and dark spirits hate it—so I'd like for us to plan an evening of fastin' from refreshments, and instead feed hearty upon the Word and worshipin' in word 'n song. We'll have pauses between singin' so that we all can share whatever 'tis the Spirit moves us to utter for our own and others' benefit."

"Praise God!" Molly and Marissa murmured, the twins clasping hands in a special union of prayer.

"Scripture says that there's rejoicin' in heaven every time a soul is turned from its evil ways. Well, why not a little bit of hoorahing 'n happiness here on earth, too! We promised our men a coverin' of prayer—well, ladies, I think we could have our own little Grant Hotel revival this very evenin'!"

"We'll rattle the rafters!" Alice Meloney predicted.

"Lord willin', we sure will," Lizzie agreed. "Rose's baby grand piano is over there gatherin' dust. Any of you womenfolk got the abilities so's you could play a few tunes 'n dust off the keys for me at the same time?"

Lizzie's playfully worded suggestion was met with appreciative laughter as womenfolk regarded each other.

"Alice, I know you played," Stella Jensen, Lars' wife, reminded the wealthy lumber company owner's wife, who'd arrived a few minutes after she had.

"But it's been ages!"

"Reckon that onct you learned how, you don't completely forget it!" Lizzie encouraged.

"But I'll be so rusty!" Alice protested.

"I ain't done much hymn singing since Sunday services. My voice'll be rusty, too!" Lizzie pointed out. She clapped her hands. "C'mon, girls! What do you say? Let's all knock the rust off ourselves together! Alice, iffen you'll shake the cobwebs from your piano talents, we'll do the same with our voices. Why, by night's end, we'll sound like heavenly choirs!"

"It's for a good cause!" Joy quietly spoke up.

"Anyone have any special requests?" Alice inquired as she made her way to the piano.

"'Onward Christian Soldiers'!"

"How about 'Victory in Jesus'? I always liked that 'un."

"Let's not forget 'Old Rugged Cross,' girls!"

"Of course not! And being as our men are facing what they are tonight, I think we could rest our singing voices for a moment by joining together in a special prayer for Lolly Ravachek and then singing 'What a Friend We Have in Jesus'!"

"Oh—that idea's inspired, Lydia! I just got goose bumps!"

Alice Meloney gave Rose Ames' metronome a little tap to set it into motion, played an intro, then turned toward the cluster of Williams women collected around the piano, and within thirty seconds all the rust was banished to reveal pure gold, fit for presentation to a heavenly King.

The confusing and ominous dark of night was forced to give way to diamond-brilliant dawn that would not be denied. It was a fresh morning before the Christian women's husky voices faded away on the final song, 'Victory in Jesus,' which they'd sung time and time again, as they believed in the Lord and in what their men and they themselves were doing as they gathered together in Christian agreement for Lolly Ravachek's salvation and redemption.

Windows at the Grant Hotel were open to let in the balmy evening air, and the strains of the well-loved hymns drifted through the night to where a small knot of grim-faced, determined men stood outside the Black Diamond Saloon, what the pastor had long considered a "tar paper den of iniquity!"

It was clear that Lolly Ravachek was inside, unabashedly reading fortunes through the week, even though come Sunday she would like as not position herself in a pew.

"If she's interested in followin' the Lord, then she's got to make a choice," Brad said.

"It's our Christian duty to exhort one we believe is in ignorance of God's way," the pastor said.

"What do we do? Hie on in and haul her out?" Lester asked, the tension in his form conveying that he was ready for action.

"It's a matter of will," the pastor reminded. "Miss Ravachek has been involved in this through her own free will, even if there has been the taint of intergenerational bondage inherited in her bloodline, due to ancestors making pacts with ungodly forces."

"In other words?. . .," Brad prompted.

"We ask Lolly to come out and meet with us."

"If she does?"

"Then we may get underway."

"If she refuses?"

"Then we go home—a confrontation canceled, unless she should show up at worship services."

"Then we'd have no choice but to chastise her."

"And it'd be a heap more powerful than simply the testimony of two men, for we've all been witness to this travesty."

Quickly the men prayed, then sent in a request, with a person about to enter the tar paper shack, that they wished to see Miss Ravachek.

To their surprise, she came right out. Her face was flushed, her spirits high, and it was clear she'd been having an enjoyable—and profitable—evening.

"What can I do for you?" she asked in a mannerly tone, looking with confusion from grim face to somber expression.

"You can cease your dark deeds and evil behaviors, Ma'am," Lester began. "No faultin' you, Lolly, for as a human bein', you're likable enough—"

"But your behaviors are an abomination," the pastor took over.

Lolly listened, stunned, as the men talked on, first one, then another, until her head felt woozy and swirling with the agonizing, spiraling, conflicting thought patterns.

Pastor Edgerton sensed what was afoot.

"Would you agree to accompany us to the parsonage so we can talk for a spell in more comfortable surroundings?"

Lolly seemed suspended in a moment that stretched out to eternity.

"Please?" Lester softly added.

"Very well," she agreed.

"Come along with us, Miss Lolly," Pastor Edgerton gently urged, gripping her arm.

"My—"

"Mr. Mathews will accept possession of your belongings— don't worry."

"All . . . right . . .," Lolly said.

She was led along in the darkness, as if she were in a coma.

It wasn't until they neared the parsonage that suddenly she issued forth with a baying, inhumane scream and began to snarl and scratch and hiss like a furious demonic beast.

"In the name of Jesus Christ, who shed his blood on Calvary for this poor woman, demon, I command you to be silent!" Pastor Edgerton thundered.

"Lord in heaven!. . .," Brad whispered.

He'd heard of such things, wasn't sure if he had fully believed in them, at least not as a condition in the world at the moment but perhaps only as a situation from the days when the Lord walked on earth, healing those possessed with demons and evil spirits.

"Protect us, Jesus," Lester implored over and over under his breath.

"I claim the Lord Jesus Christ's blood as my protection!" Sven fearlessly announced to the forces he couldn't see—but could *feel.* He knew that regardless of what mistakes he'd made in the past, and what error-filled paths he'd once trodden, at that moment, and for all eternity, he knew that he was on the right side, in the Lord's kingdom, and he desperately wished for Lolly Ravachek, a helpless captive, to know that same liberation that came through freedom gained by accepting her Lord and Savior.

No one had expected the altercation to be over in a matter of moments, but neither had they anticipated that the physical and spiritual exertions would be more exhausting than an arduous day spent hard at work in the deep timber.

They'd known Lolly, but as the pastor commanded the dark spirits within her, they realized it wasn't a mere human being that they were contending with—it was dank and depraved powers. In the same way, they knew it wasn't their own human strengths that were commanding the situation—they were worshipfully aware of the very power of the Holy Spirit filling the room until it was driving out the dreadful and destructive demon forces.

One by one demons were being released, ordered to identify themselves and those that they were bound to, and then power groups were cast from Lolly Ravachek and ordered to go to the foot of the cross, face Jesus, and do what he commanded them to do, and not send other demonic spirits in their place.

The men quailed inwardly, even though their faith was strong, as Lolly writhed, screamed, wretched, coughed, and was thrown about the room and into almost humanly impossible contortions during the worst throes while Pastor Edgerton and the Christian men, aided by their believing wives and children across town at the Grant Hotel, took authority in Christ's name over the principalities and powers that had threatened the town and its people.

At the saloon, Lolly had been an exotic beauty of hardened, glittery countenance. As the night progressed, the men felt as if they'd witnessed her destruction—but then realized it was the removal of demons and that instead they were witnessing a rebirth of the spirit when Lolly was freed of demon forces so that her will became stronger and stronger.

Soon she was able to help the men, woozily but oh-so-willingly renouncing her past associations and dark alliances, breaking ancient covenants of her family with Satan's fallen angels, claiming Christ's blood to wash away fraudulent deals with the Father of Lies, as God's promise would stand forever.

It was an exhausted but cleansed Lolly Ravachek who collapsed against Pastor Edgerton. He steadied her and then, nodding to Brad and Lester, eased her toward the sofa, where she wilted as if in a faint. Tears were streaming down her cheeks, but they were no longer tears of hate and anguish—they were tears of joy that she'd been washed clean of her past and born anew, at her age and on that date, into God's kingdom.

Pastor Edgerton helped Lolly frame a confession of faith, and she gained strength and in her own words fervently committed her life to Jesus Christ, her Lord and Savior.

The men whom Lolly had screamed at, railing horrible, vile oaths, she now regarded with gentle love and gratitude that was shining in her eyes, which were red-rimmed from crying.

"Thank you so much," she whispered. "I can never thank you enough."

"You don't owe us any kind o' debt, Miss Lolly," Brad said. "Everything any of us have, are, or can be—we owe to the Lord. He gave his life on the cross for us—and in accepting that he paid the full price on our accounts, then's when we give our lives to him so his Spirit can reside 'n work in us. . . ."

chapter
12

"I THINK THEY'RE back!" someone said when there were heavy footfalls on the front stoop of the Grant Hotel.

Lizzie rushed across the lobby, with a gaggle of tired women on her heels. She threw open the door just as Pastor Edgerton moved ahead to open it. Brad and Lester were supporting between them a bedraggled Lolly Ravachek, who looked nothing like the chic and attractive woman who'd turned heads around town.

When she looked at Lizzie, there was a different cast to her gaze, a soft glow from eyes reddened with many tears. She wilted against the men who supported her, as if there were no strength left in her. Clearly, the woman was drained.

"She needs to rest," Brad said.

"Can you . . . Can she . . .," Lizzie looked dubiously toward the curving staircase.

"Have we got an empty room, Ma?" Lester inquired.

"Well . . . yes. . . ." Lizzie's hesitant response bore witness that she was confused because Lolly already had a room.

"Her occult articles and items she used in strange rituals and witchcraft are in that room," Pastor Edgerton said. "The vulnerable state she's in right now, she shouldn't be put in a room with such tainted items."

"Right you are!" Lizzie said. Understanding flowed over her, and scriptural texts came to mind to verify the need.

Lizzie saw to getting Lolly tucked into fresh quarters on the ground floor, where they could keep an eye on her. Joy and some of the menfolk's women hurriedly worked in the kitchen to prepare a meal to feed the famished church members who'd been up through the night.

Two hours later red-eyed people had all departed for their homes, and Lizzie set the last freshly cleaned and dried dish in the cabinet. Already, food on the range was sending off rich aromas from the succulent meats and vegetables cooking for the dinnertime crowd.

"Come have a cup of coffee, sweetheart," Brad said. "It's all poured, creamed, and waitin'."

"That sounds wonderful. I ain't sat down a'tall since dawn. I'm tired."

"We're all exhausted," Brad quietly stated.

"I'm glad that's over," Lizzie said.

" . . . Don't know iffen it's over. . . . But at least it's begun."

Lizzie looked startled.

"But I gathered that Lolly accepted the Lord," Lizzie said. "That after y'all confronted her and explained to her what she'd been a-doin' all o' her life and read Scripture and testi- fied, Lolly suffered conviction, repented, and opened her heart to the Lord and accepted him into her life."

"That she did," Brad said, nodding solemnly. "But Pastor Edgerton also had to impress upon her that although now she has new life in Christ and he'll be with her always, Satan's fallen angels are going to torment her in every way possible if they've a legal right from old involvements and unrepented sins."

"What do you mean?" Lizzie asked, even though she had a crawly sense that she'd almost be happier not knowing.

"The Devil has lost Lolly Ravachek to the Lord's kingdom. He's going to want her back. As much as was accomplished in the last twenty-four hours, 'tis just the first day of Lolly's new life as a Christian. There are no doubt a lot o' dark corners that need to be swept out 'n cleaned up to allow the light of the Lord to shine freely, exposing all so that it can be given up to him. From what the preacher says, it's sort of like having offal hanging around to draw opossums 'n other scavenging varmints. As long as there's something gamy there, they'll keep swoopin' in to try 'n feast on it. But get rid of the offal that attracts 'em, and they end up with no reason nor room to come around."

"Kind of a countrified way of puttin' it," Lizzie said. "But it makes sense."

"With the involvement she's been in, Satan's going to be merciless. The preacher says that to his knowledge, in such cases involvin' the occult, witchcraft, 'n such, it's a tough walk for a new believer. They get hit incredibly hard as Satan tries to win 'em back to him . . . with trickery, doubt, deceit, confusion, curiosity, masqueradin' as the purest good, usin' fondest of friends, old and new, and what-have-you to try to snag her and purchase a hold again."

A shudder went through Lizzie when she considered how in Scripture a person had been delivered of evil spirits, the dark forces were sent out, roamed, but later returned, bringing spirits even worse with them. The demons had found the premises clean and moved in to take over again.

"That poor girl!" Lizzie said with sudden fearful understanding of what they all faced.

"She warrants our pity, and she needs our prayers," Brad agreed. "But we also must be firm with Lolly—for her good and for our own. The preacher says that Satan's a sore loser. He won't give up easily—especially not on one who's unknowingly been in his service so many years and is an apparent victim of intergenerational bondage."

"Brad, you're confusin' me . . .," Lizzie tiredly protested, cupping her head in her hands.

He patted his weary wife's hand. "We're *all* tired 'n confused. The pastor'd like a passle o' us to come to the parsonage this evenin' so's he can supply us with explanations, Scripture texts, 'n we can pray over the matter."

"We'll be there," Lizzie grimly said.

"Someone will have to stay with Lolly," he pointed out.

"That'll be arranged."

"We menfolk are hopin' that after she rests up a bit today, we can join together, go to her quarters, pray for her protection, help her to renounce her witchcraft involvements, and, as the folks long ago did and is detailed in the Acts of the Apostles, have her rid herself of the items by burnin' and destroyin' them to free her of their tainting bondage."

"She's got a powerful lot of possessions," Lizzie said.

"She'd be wise to get shed of all of it," Brad murmured. "But we don't know iffen we can quite ask that of her— clothes and all. We're going to prayerfully guide her over things that we *know* have to go—'n ask the Lord to open our eyes to things that would be displeasing in his sight."

"This is like a nightmare, Brad, ain't it?" Lizzie said.

"It's not like we ain't read o' such things in the Good Book," he pointed out.

"But it was almost, at times, like some of that didn't really apply to . . . *today*. Just doesn't seem that such dark and destructive things should be happenin' on a sunny Minnesota day surrounded by nature 'n such an abundance of the Lord's creation."

"I know, Liz."

"Iffen this ain't over—how long's it goin' to last?"

"God knows," Brad admitted. "We can trust that it won't last one iota longer than the Lord deems necessary for us to learn the things set in store for us to discover by this experience, and to grow in faith and Christian unity as a result of it."

"The Word's a comfort in all of this, ain't it?" Lizzie said. She managed a smile, struggling for her usual levity. "I'm sure glad that Scripture says, 'And it came to pass' and *not* 'It came to stay'! Someday 'twill be over. . . ."

It was midafternoon when Lolly awakened, groggy but also excited about what had taken place within her. There was a joy like she had never known and a sense of cleanliness like she had not previously experienced.

"I . . . love . . . you . . . all . . .," she wearily said, smiling through her exhaustion, when the church members were clustered around her so supportively. "You're . . . good people. . . . The crystal ball sent me to Williams . . . and it was dark spirits' directives I was following without knowing that . . . but Jesus Christ knew that *you* would be awaiting me here. . . ."

Unable to restrain her joy, Lolly cast aside her pride and shared with them the horror of her life from which the Lord had saved her for his own.

"I've heard so . . . much Scripture from . . . everyone, and Pastor Edgerton gave . . . me my own Bible. . . . Now I can read it . . . for myself."

"You'll enjoy it," Lizzie assured. "Newborn infants seems to always want to nurse. You'll be takin' in the milk o' Scripture, and before we all know it, you'll be a mature believer ready to digest the meat o' the Word."

"You're aware of what needs to be done, aren't you, Lolly?" Pastor Edgerton gently urged.

" . . . Yes. . . ."

"Are you ready to begin?"

Fear momentarily passed across Lolly's tired but joyful features.

" . . . Yes. . . ."

"You are agreeing to destroy your occult objects freely? We can't force you to do it, Lolly. It must be your choice."

"I wish I'd never seen them." She drew a deep breath and seemed infused with strength. She arose and slowly but steadily approached the staircase to go to the quarters where she'd practiced her dark arts.

Joining hands as they followed Lolly, the pastor and bedrock members of his congregation softly prayed for Lolly's protection and their own as she rid her life of her possessions and rejected the forces that had controlled her for all of her days.

A splitting out, splintery, willow laundry basket that had seen better days was donated by Lizzie Mathews to contain the offensive articles that could be taken to a nearby field and smashed and burned by Lolly Ravachek as the believers prayed in faith.

"Lord, open our eyes," Pastor Edgerton said, "that we may see what is an offense and abomination to you and remove it from our presence and reject it from your child Lolly Ravachek's life. Help her to freely abandon any objects displeasing to you, and empower us to assist her in closing forbidden doors that have been opened in her life."

"Amen . . .," the believers softly chorused.

Grim-lipped, determined, Lolly quickly began to scrabble around her room, tossing item after item into the basket with disdain.

The burdensome load began to mount in the basket, and

when it was filled to brimming, Lizzie whisked a pillow slip from the feather pillow and wordlessly handed it to the pastor, who held it open for Lolly so she could continue to deposit her items.

"I think that's everything," Lolly said.

The minutes had passed in a blur for her. She'd hardly been aware of all she'd kept—and what she'd discarded—sometimes seeking her new friends' counsel as she tried to reach a conclusion.

When she finished, she had almost nothing left save a few clothes that she hadn't worn while performing dark rituals, and the new, black, leather-bound Bible that she'd carried with her.

Lolly did a quick doublecheck, then was satisfied.

"That's everything," she whispered, glancing around, satisfied.

"Let us pray . . .," the pastor suggested, then intoned a fervent prayer before they filed down the staircase, out into an abandoned field, and Lolly smashed and burned the offensive objects. Then the menfolk helped her bury the remains.

Lizzie, moved by the courage she'd seen in Lolly, put her arm around her and gave her a warm hug.

"You're a brave girl, honey," she said. "And you've just made the most important decision of your life today. You won't regret it! Sometimes people who've wallowed in evil are the ones who end up most cherishin' and understanding the goodness and mercy of the Lord."

"I've hardly anything left!. . .," Lolly mused, awed.

"The Lord'll provide all you need," Lizzie said. "Generous and God-fearing folks live in this town. You won't be abandoned."

"Lolly Ravachek is going to need us as she's never needed people around her before," the pastor solemnly began speaking to the assembled group of devout members of the congregation. "To understand what Lolly faces, and as her supporters, you need to have a basic grasp of a condition known as intergenerational bondage. It's a term one doesn't often hear, as a matter of fact, so don't be upset if it's new to you. . . ."

With that, the pastor began speaking, regularly reading Scriptures from the Old Testament that dealt with fortune-telling, soothsaying, divining, and other abominations practiced in the worship of Baal, which angered the Lord.

"'I, the Lord your God, am a jealous God, punishing the children for the sin of the fathers to the third and fourth generation of those who hate me, but showing love to thousands who love me and keep my commandments.'"

The pastor paused a moment. "Think on that verse, my friends, and consider Lolly's plight. This's a turning point, not only in her life but for generations of her future lineage. What we've been part of was fearsome, to be sure, but it was also an honor and an education for us all to have our Lord use us as he has, and it is to be an education that will no doubt deepen and illuminate Scripture verses forevermore."

There were many nods and a heavy silence as he let the words penetrate the minds of those gathered together.

"For generations, Lolly Ravachek's family has been involved in occultic practices. She and her ancestors have willingly taken part in rituals forbidden by God and warned of as abominable in his sight. Lolly was born into such a family. She was tainted before birth by the sin of her ancestors.

"It is known that in families where there is a history of occultic bondage, these dark powers and evil spirits pass from generation to generation, and therefore Lolly would have inherited her unusual abilities. Because she did, she assumed that such talents were God-given, when nothing was farther from the truth."

By the time an hour had passed, Lizzie, Brad, and the others assembled had a solid knowledge of what had warped Lolly's life, and they were moved with sympathy and compassion, knowing that she was helpless over having been born into such a lineage but that the Lord in his mercy had sent her to them that she might be salvaged.

"There's a warning in Matthew 12:43–45 that it will require much steadfastness for Lolly to live a strong Christian life. We must assist her as brothers and sisters in Christ so that she can stand strong, not fall into weakness and be fooled by evil tricks and temptations so that she falls away and her last state is worse than her first. . . ."

"We'll do all that we can," the church members vowed.

"We can do what we are able to be supportive and to encourage her to be strong in the Lord, and edify her with our understanding of the Word. But the final choice . . . is Lolly's. And we must pray that in the diabolical attacks she will undoubtedly face—and the temptations and beguiling tricks she will be confronted with to make evil appear good, and good evil—she will be discerning."

chapter
13

THAD CHILDERS HAD noticed that the farther north the barge progressed along the Mississippi River, the thinner the humidity seemed, and the air was drenched with a refreshing pine scent. The river bluffs were different, too, faced with outcroppings of limestone to which tenacious evergreens managed to grow in crevices, precariously reaching out for the sun, their roots solidly clinging to crannies in the soft stone.

Since signing on with the barge company, Thad had worked hard and played little. When the barge was docked to unload cargo and take on freight to go farther upriver, he'd shouldered his share of the work. When his barge mates eagerly scrambled onto solid ground and set out to sample the diversions offered in teeming river cities, Thad generally returned to his quarters.

Asked to accompany them, Thad had politely declined, unwilling to squander his time and money in such useless pursuits again, when he had so many important things to do. Thad had worked hard and spent little of his wages. His basic needs were provided for by the barge company. Since joining the crew in the Deep South, he'd abandoned the comforting familiarity of the barge only long enough to go on brief forays into several river cities along the route.

The first time, he'd purchased a brand-new Bible, and after

that he'd left the barge only to replenish his supplies of writing paper and pencils.

"Ya ain't much of a talker," the barge captain had once teased him, "but you're sure a writin' fool, ain't ya?"

"Reckon so," Thad had said, smiling thoughtfully, his pencil poised against the tablet.

"What're you wantin' to do? Be like that Mark Twain feller who hailed from way back down 'round Hannibal?"

"Nothin' like that," Thad said, chuckling, but he didn't explain his behaviors.

Thad realized that after being what his ma had called a "chatterbox" when he was a child, in recent months he had become quiet in a self-absorbed way as he struggled to recall just who he was, where he'd been, what he'd done, and figure out where he was meant to go in life.

Although he was aware that his mind was healing and improving, he did not yet trust his memory, and therefore when the events returned for his recall, he felt burdened to write down the knowledge so it'd never escape him so completely again. It had been harrowing to be lost in a murky void where thought had no measure of meaning.

And quickly he'd discovered that when he wrote down the events from his life, like keeping a latter-day diary, upon rereading what he'd recalled and set to paper, it was rather like priming a pump. One memory seemed to kindle another . . . which lit another . . . which caused yet a different thought to flare up in his mind . . . and as a result, he had a heightened illumination of just who he'd been in life.

With the Good Book to guide him again, he felt an increased sense of godly direction in where the Lord intended for him to go that he might live in conjunction with the will of God.

"Sure am goin' to hate to lose you, Son," the barge captain

said when he happened upon Thad, who was sitting in the sunlight and enjoying the beautiful northern Midwestern summer day now that the long journey was almost over.

"I've enjoyed the trip, sir," Thad said.

"You've been my best worker. Wisht that I had a whole crew like you."

"You've got some good men, though . . .," Thad said.

"That I do. But not as good as you, Thad."

"Thank you. It's nice to be appreciated."

"You've got a job with this barge line anytime you've a notion," the captain said. "Keep it in mind!"

"I will, sir," Thad promised. "I'm not exactly sure what I'll be doing, other than going farther north for a spell to visit with my fam'bly."

"They're no doubt anticipatin' your arrival."

" . . . They don't know I'm on my way. . . ."

"Well, won't that be a jim-dandy, humdinger o' a surprise, then!"

"Hope so."

"The way you're writin' all the time, kind o' startles me that you ain't dropped 'em a note to let 'em know you're on your way."

" . . . Guess it slipped my mind," Thad dismissed, not wanting to discuss the fact that he'd felt hesitant about the matter and had frequently turned to the story of the Prodigal Son in the New Testament to reassure himself that his blood kin would be as happy about his return to them as he sensed that the Lord was pleased that he'd come back to the fold after a walk on the wild side that had taught him a lot about things of true value in life.

"What're you doin'? Writin' your life story?" the captain pressed a bit more.

" . . . Somethin' like that," Thad admitted. "Just scribblin' down a lot of fond and funny memories from my past."

"And some of them not so fond and funny, likely," the captain said. "I reckon we appreciate recallin' the fond and funny times because they're such a cherished relief from the terrible and tragic occurrences."

"That's true enough. . . ."

"I could sure tell the world a lot o' stories," the captain softly mused.

Thad smiled and waved a sheaf of papers at his boss. "No one's stoppin' you," he said. "Maybe you're the one to make Mark Twain move over, aye?"

"That takes time, and as captain o' this barge, time's often one thing I don't have enough of. And when I do—I reckon I don't have the discipline to do it, like you seem to. Tell you what, though, Thaddie—iffen you ever feel an urge to drop me a line in care of the barge company, you take the time to write 'n I'll sure delight in using a bit o' time to read correspondence from you."

"I'll do that, sir," Thad said. "Promise."

"Mayhap I'll write back to you," the captain said, "'specially if I think I can lure you back into my employ."

"Might happen," Thad said. "I do like workin' the waterways, that I know."

"And you're good at it," the captain said. "Almost like ya got seawater in your veins! Stay in touch, mate!"

"I will. . . ."

Talking about his near future plans during the brief conversation with his captain made them seem all the more real to Thad. He was still a goodly distance from Williams, Minnesota—he had pinpointed the location on the map, recalling that his ma and Brad had ventured up there to run a hotel for a woman whose name still escaped him.

Sometime later it had returned to his mind that Lester and Harmony had decided to resettle up north, too, although it was still hazy in his memory if they'd headed north first or if Ma and Brad had.

Thad no longer tortured himself in trying to sort out such minor details. They weren't that important. And he sensed that someday everything would fall into place.

He couldn't help believing that when he arrived in Williams and saw his family, there would be many episodes from his life that would become clear. And if not, the very people who had spent so many years with him in the cabin near Salt Creek could serve as his memory.

No doubt they could tell him who he was and just who he'd been, in addition to what he'd already recalled. And unless he missed his guess, the stories that they could remind him of would prime the pump for more of his own recollections to come gushing out.

How good it would be to see them, he thought as his pencil rested against the paper. He leaned back and sunlight bathed his face, his eyes closed against the bright, searing touch.

His mama and Brad . . .

Lester . . .

Harmony . . .

A lot of time had passed since he'd been smack-dab in the middle of the family fold. He'd changed drastically. He was wondering how they'd changed, too, although he contented himself that some things would never be different.

His mama'd be cooking up a storm while Brad lovingly watched her or assisted her in her labors or tended to his own.

No doubt Les was still crazy in love with horses and mules, mayhap even owned a goodly number himself.

And Harmony?

"Bet her nose is still in a book . . .," Thad whispered to himself and smiled. "Bein' a librarian and gettin' paid to do what she loves. . . ."

He knew that on the barge, he was being paid to do what he loved, and he almost hated to leave the cargo company's employ, but the pull of family bonds drove him on.

He knew that he'd leave the barge and the river with an inner longing to return to a life somewhere on the water. But he'd stay with family, that was for sure, until he knew it was the Lord's will, not his own, beguiling him to move on to where he was meant to be. . . .

Pitt, Minnesota

"To look at us," Lester Childers said, glancing at his brother-in-law, Billy, and his stepfather, Brad, "no one would ever guess that we were totin' such a load of jack in this ol' wagon."

"Doesn't take a very big tote sack of gold to make a sizable sum," Brad yawned.

"I'm enjoying this day as I've relished few days since Harmony's passin'."

Lester grinned. "I reckon Brad 'n I'll savor it almost as much as you do."

"I want you both there!" Billy said.

"Dressed just as we are."

"Of course."

"I'll guarantee that banker's chin's goin' to drop down and bang against his fancy desk when you hie on in there, dressed in your old buckskins 'n trappin' garb, produce that little sack, up-end it, and gold pieces clatter all over his desk—and you ask to open up an account."

"Wonder if he'll loan me any money after this?" Billy mused.

"Pro'bly be trippin' over himself offerin' you extry funds iffen you want 'em or need 'em."

"Actually, I hope he does," Billy said. "I've got capital but big plans too, and that takes a lot of money."

"You're a good investment, Son," Brad assured.

"We're going to have a bit of fun with the banker man," Billy said. "But I'm hoping that I'll be able to consider him my friend. A businessman needs such contacts."

"Keep in mind that he could use a depositor like you, too, Billy," Lester said.

"I ain't no fortune-teller," Brad said, "but I've always had this feelin' that you were goin' to be an important man in this area, Bill. Well, at least that's the feelin' I got after Harmony took up with you 'n you straightened up and walked right."

"Speakin' of fortune-tellers, how's it going with Lolly?" Lester inquired. "I'm half hesitant to even broach the topic with her or Ma, figurin' I might be happier not knowin'."

"She's come a long ways in a short time," Billy said.

"It seems to us, from what Lolly's said, that the oppression is easin' up some, at least to my understandin' o' the situation," Brad said, then added, "Lolly 'n Liz have become a lot closer than I'd have ever believed would happen, the way that strange girl set Liz's teeth on edge from the moment they met."

"Ma's always been intuitive," Lester said. "She senses things. But in a good and godly way—not like Lolly ended up knowin' the things that she knew."

"That's because your ma's always been led by the Spirit of God, and her knowledge and knowin' comes from him, one o' the gifts of the Spirit. The ol' Devil is a counterfeiter from way back. So folks aligned with his ways, whether they know it or not, possess a counterfeit gift that instead of edifyin' them in the Lord, eases them toward destruction.

"The preacher says that when the weird knowin' hits Lolly, she's got to recognize where it's a-comin' from, know that it's dark forces trying to tempt and trick her back into usin' those abilities, so she's gotta close those doors and shut 'em forever with the redeeming, protective blood of Jesus, which cancels out 'n nullifies any pledge her lineage of kin has cast with the Evil One in generations past."

"Pastor Edgerton's been a major blessin' in all of this," Lester said.

"When you think back how he ended up in town, was here so many times when he was exactly what we needed, and was a perfect man of God to deal with this situation with Lolly—well, we was all viewin' miracles in the makin'.'"

"When he received a callin' to come to Williams, obviously it was the Lord leadin' him to us, knowin' that one day we'd have a powerful need for Pastor Edgerton."

"He's gone above and beyond in working with Miss Lolly, having Bible studies with her, explaining to her the things she needs to know about this intergenerational bondage. And his Lydia couldn't have been more supportive. Levi's sure warmed up to Miss Lolly, too. She's as dear as an aunt to the little feller."

"Nice too the way the young mothers 'round town have taken to hiring Lolly to help 'em with odds and ends so's she has a little money comin' in."

"The church people will see to it that she won't have any need to ever turn back to her fortune-tellin' ways to provide a roof over her head or put food in her mouth."

"There's a serious risk she'll turn back . . . ain't there?" Lester said. "Even though she seems fine right now."

Grim silence filled the air around them, broken only by the soft creak of wooden wagon wheels, the twitch of the horses' tails at flies, and an impatient snort as the team realized they were drawing near to the rebuilt town of Baudette.

"I reckon all o' us prefer not to think about it," Brad finally spoke, "but . . . yes. We know what temptations is in our lives . . . it's worse for Miss Lolly. She was in the dark kingdom for so long, and Satan wants her back, even by default iffen she ain't his anymore but he can dupe her into backslidin' to ineffectiveness. And iffen he can't get her back handily enough . . . he'll want her dead. . . ."

Billy shrugged. "He wants all of us dead. Once we have new life in Christ, we're basically useless to him, so he'd prefer we were out of the way before we encourage others to find the same pathway of escape that we've received in the Lord."

"I've never quite thought of it like that," Brad said. "But you're right."

"Sounds like you've given the subject more than a little thought," Lester observed.

"I guess I have," Billy admitted. "With Harmony gone and evenings so lonely, sometimes there's nothing to do except sit close to the coal oil lamp, read the Good Book . . .'n think. Seems to me that when we're born anew in Christ, since we're no longer spiritually dead because of what happened with Adam and Eve in the garden when they forfeited everything good that the Lord had given to them, then the Evil One wants a person physically dead and out of his way here on earth and does all he can to achieve that result."

"That's true enough. And he can cause a heap o' misery and sufferin' in the process."

"But if the Lord's got a hedge around a person, Satan's barred from causing death 'til the Lord's ready to call that person home because their earthly work is over. . . . Like Harmony. And someday Lizzie."

"Satan's battered her awfully hard over the years," Brad admitted.

Billy smiled tenderly. "That's 'cause Ma's such a thorn in his side, loving people, doing unto the least as if she were doing it for the Lord himself."

"And Ma won't stop, either," Lester said. "When she knows that evil forces surround her, that's when she comes out a-sluggin' with Scripture, prayer, and a faith that grows stronger each time it's buffeted 'n blown around."

"Sounds like you've got some observations worth sharing," Brad said. "Sure sparked some lively, edifyin' conversation just now."

"Be glad to when we've got the time," Billy said.

"We'll be holdin' you to that," Lester declared as he stopped the horses and wagon in front of the bank on Main Street.

Billy hopped down, the sack of gold merrily jingling as he landed on the sidewalk.

"Right now we've got business to attend to!"

Williams, Minnesota

"Back from helpin' Lydia, are you?" Lizzie sang out when Lolly returned to the hotel. "Just about in time for dinner!"

"And it smells delicious!"

Lizzie glanced at the grandfather clock. "As early as the men left—before dawn—they should be arrivin' in Baudette directly."

Lolly sensed that they were already there. But she did not admit as much. She was aware of the risky situation that she was in, and she knew that the townspeople were alarmed on her behalf. She'd caused them quite enough problems without needlessly frightening them that her powers were back and at work.

Didn't everyone sometimes have the urges and intuition? Surely such thoughts and impressions didn't mean a return of the dark abilities that Pastor Edgerton had warned she would have to be wary might steal back, perhaps trying to confuse her that her knowledge might be the bona fide gift of the Spirit, which would be used to assist and comfort Christian friends.

"Wisht I knew how it was goin' for 'em," Lizzie spoke thirty minutes later.

"Surely it'll work out just fine," Lolly assured. "After all, this time Billy's returning a quite rich man."

Neither of them spoke about the fact that he'd journeyed to Massacre Island, found his long-lost cache of gold, only because of Lolly's odd awarenesses.

"They're goin' to be plumb tuckered out when they return tonight, makin' the trip all in one day like they plan. And Will plans on headin' out to the lake come break o' day."

" . . . Is Serenity going with him to visit her people?" Lolly casually asked.

Lizzie whisked the back of her hand across her brow to capture a bead of sweat and didn't look toward Lolly to see the girl carefully avoiding even a chance fleeting connection with Lizzie's gaze.

"Don't rightly know," she said. "She hasn't said anything about it. Now that she's been keepin' a bit of company with Sven Larsen, she doesn't seem to trek to the lakeside with Will as regularly as she used to."

"I'd noticed that."

The two women fell silent, the conversation seeming over.

Lizzie was helpless not to think about the changes in Serenity, how there'd been times she seemed like hunted quarry with her predator only a breath away from pouncing. Normally a friendly and accepting person, the best that Serenity could express in Lolly's direction was the most tepid of lukewarm behavior.

"Surprisin', ain't it?" Lizzie blurted the question when her thoughts flew back over recent months and fully compiled the list of outward and inward changes that suddenly seemed especially confusing. "I think everyone in town had realized that Serenity was sweet on Will, even if he wasn't fully apprised of the fact. And it was pretty clear that Will certainly held Serenity in high regard, even if he was too lonesome 'n wounded to think of her in terms other than just a dear friend of our departed Harmony."

" . . . Maybe Serenity tired of waiting for William to notice her?" Lolly casually suggested.

"I don't know about that. Serenity ain't just a calm and peaceful girl—she's also patient."

"She must have her reasons," Lolly said.

"Reckon she does. But as silent as she is about her own business, won't be no one else but the Lord aware of what they are 'til Serenity chances to tell 'em. . . ."

Lolly felt needled with guilt. She never had felt a need, or taken the initiative, to apologize to Serenity and ask her forgiveness and assure her that there was no ill will remaining.

She'd noticed that since she threatened Serenity with the revelation of her part in Harmony LeFave's death from diphtheria, the pretty Indian girl had grown more silent. She was never impolite to Lolly, but she gave her wide berth.

And after that, Serenity had ceased looking at William LeFave, almost as if it caused the Indian girl physical pain to gaze upon him, so she'd deflected her sight from him and focused on Sven Larsen, who was delighted to obtain the pretty, dark-haired girl's attention.

It was clear that Serenity and Sven were friends and that he was terribly fond of her, but in that deep and dark place, Lolly knew that Serenity wasn't in love with Sven. Lolly *knew* that Serenity was still in love with William, as Lolly also considered herself to be.

Lolly knew that William held her in high regard. He always was polite and gallant, respectful, and all the things that she could wish for in a man, including being possessed of dark and dashing good looks.

Nowadays she was helpless not to idly wonder if William was the one intended for her. She'd come to see her dark force involvements for what they were—counterfeits of the works of the Creator who was her Savior and Redeemer. But she had also seen how the Lord had used circumstances arranged by the Devil, and in the end they had wound up a gambit that eventually worked toward the Lord's will, even though the events had been dealt by dark spirits. It was true, as others stressed, that all things work toward good for those who love the Lord.

"Life's so confusing," Lolly murmured.

"Pardon?" Lizzie responded to the gypsy girl's mused comment.

"Nothing really, Lizzie. I was just pondering the past and thinking over how everything—good, bad, or seemingly inconsequential—ends up serving the Master's plan."

"That it does," Lizzie said. "Sometimes we have to live a heap longer, though, in order to look back and clearly see the wisdom of the Lord's ways as it was all unfoldin'. . . ."

"I suppose so. I'm already starting to have a clearer vision of that," Lolly said.

"That's a blessin', darlin'! The Lord's allowed a heavy cross on your shoulder."

"And I'll gladly bear it," Lolly said, "to be delivered from the taint of bondage inherited from my ancestors. . . ."

"Be thankful the Lord saved you from that, Lolly! Why, think of it—you're startin' a generation turned to the Lord! And the same chapter in Exodus that speaks of sins of the father also promises the mercy and acceptance for a thousand generations for those who love the Lord."

"We'll soon have a new member of the coming generation, from Joy," Lolly said.

"She's due anytime!" Lizzie agreed. "I wonder if it'll be a boy or a girl?"

"Just so it's healthy," Lolly said.

"Right you are!"

Lolly fell silent. She kept to herself that she'd had a dream about Joy, and in the dream, the child had been—

Stop it! she mentally ordered herself.

But she was helpless not to think to the times when she'd dangled a pendulum before a pregnant woman's belly, watched the movements—and accurately predicted the gender of the coming baby.

"Been havin' fun knittin' booties 'n such," Lizzie rattled on. "Have to wait 'til after the wee one gets here to move on to colors other'n yellow and white. We'll know soon enough iffen it's a boy or a girl. Mr. Lundsten has a fine selection of yarns in both pink and blue at the mercantile."

"We won't have to wait long," Lolly said, "and then we'll know."

"Waitin' for something you'll get an answer to directly ain't too difficult," Lizzie said. "But . . ." She gave a heavy sigh and fell silent.

"But?. . .," Lolly prompted.

In Lizzie Mathews, Lolly had discovered the mama she'd never really known, and she cherished Lizzie for her warmth, her wit, her wisdom, and all the wonderful Christian traits the older woman possessed. Having learned almost as much from Lizzie as she had from Pastor Edgerton, Lolly frequently hungered to hear the older woman speak on any and all topics.

"But what, Lizzie?" Lolly prompted again as she sliced bread and laid it in baskets lined with crisp, starchy, white linen napkins.

"What?. . . Oh, I was just thinkin', that's all—about my children."

"Lester and Harmony?"

"Uh-huh."

"But you've family back in Illinois, don't you?" Lolly pointed out.

She'd known as soon as she met Lizzie that first day long ago and Lizzie handed her the ink pen to sign the guest register and their fingertips had bumblingly made contact that Lizzie was more than the mother of Lester and the late Harmony.

"Not immediate family, no," Lizzie said. "Unless you're talkin' about Maylon. He's been gone now for many years—dead to smallpox, same as the Wheeler girls' papa."

"Maylon? I haven't heard that name before."

"I was Mama to him 'n, of course, to my Thad."

"Where's Thad? Down south somewhere?" Lolly inquired, feeling certain that perhaps 'twas Thad she'd felt so strongly about a moment before.

"He's dead, and if he was found by someone and they were moved to give him a decent Christian burial, I expect that's where his remains are restin'—down south," Lizzie said.

"That's one o' those things I'll not know 'til I'm called to glory myself!. . ."

With that prompting, as she stirred gravy and dolloped pats of butter to melt over vegetables, Lizzie explained how Maylon had come to be woven into the fabric of their family's life. She sketched in what had happened to Thad.

Lizzie had declared him dead. But when she wiped a tear from her eye, fumbled for a locket, snapped it open, and revealed a lock of burnished brown hair—Thad's—which Lolly had instinctively reached out and touched with her fingertip, a psychometric jolt so strong that it was almost knifing her revealed that Thad wasn't dead—he was alive and on his way north!

Dare she tell Lizzie? Lolly knew how happy that would make her. She almost spoke, but then she realized that instead of being elated, Lizzie would be agonized, growing fearful that Lolly was about to fall under dark attack again.

And what if it was more tricks and deceits? What if Thad was really dead, a reality Lizzie had adjusted to, and Lolly gave her cruel and false hope that he yet lived and that she'd see her son again one day?

As Lizzie spoke and Lolly touched the utensils that had become Lizzie's, she felt almost jolting sensations, and to her alarm she was so shaken that she almost cast down the sharp butcher knife she was using to methodically lop off slice after slice of fresh bread . . . recognizing the almost electric sear of psychometric currents ricocheting in her body.

She knew!

It was so strong that it simply couldn't be falsity and deception. Was it knowledge given of the Lord that she might use her odd powers as a gift to comfort a Christian woman so dear to her and one who'd suffered so much?

Now Lolly knew why there was an aura of sadness about Lizzie. She had accepted Thad's death, but she still mourned over the unknown . . . knowing that there was no way to learn the comforting truth. . . . Lizzie knew comfort in an awareness of where Maylon's earthly body lay. How much greater would be her relief to know about Thad, where he lay if he'd been called from this life, or where he was if by some miracle he yet lived!

Lizzie helplessly released another heavy sigh, and Lolly knew the unspoken depth of Lizzie's private despair.

"I'm so sorry," Lolly said. She instinctively laid down the bread knife, crossed to touch Lizzie's shoulder in a gesture of sympathetic compassion.

When her skin grazed Lizzie's, the jolt intensified.

Lolly knew what she should do!

Pastor Edgerton had well informed her, warning her that dark spirits would repeatedly appear, trying to reenter the life that she'd swept clean, and, if she didn't guard against it, bring others of the same ilk and worse to inhabit the old areas, attempting to stymie her walk as a new Christian.

Lolly felt herself weaken and waver.

Lizzie turned around, concern in her eyes.

"Darlin', are you all right?"

" . . . Yes. . . ."

"You looked plumb ghastly there for a moment!" Lizzie blurted.

"I—I feel a bit . . . weak. . . ."

Lizzie's hand flew to Lolly's forehead. "You don't seem too warm—'n I can't smell a fever—"

"I'm probably just hungry," Lolly excused. "I didn't take time for breakfast. And in the kitchen, with the food smelling so good—"

"You sit down and rest a moment," Lizzie eased Lolly into a chair, "'n I'll bring you a plate of food."

Lizzie was as good as her word. Lolly picked up her fork, ate slowly and with apparent enjoyment, although she hardly tasted the food because her mind was suddenly noisy with a cacophony of thoughts that tangled and vied for her focused attention.

"Delicious dinner, Lizzie," Lolly excused herself when she had finished. "Anything you need help with? I'll be glad to assist."

"You just hie on up to your room 'n take a nap, darlin'. You're lookin' a bit peaked. Serenity and I can handle it. Iffen you're feelin' better late afternoon, then we'll see how you are and if we need you."

Slowly and carefully, feeling oddly lightheaded and almost queasy, Lolly climbed the staircase and went down the hall to the small room she'd moved into some weeks earlier because it was more affordable over the long haul.

Lolly was tired, and she believed that she'd soon fall asleep, but instead her head swam and was filled with chaotic images that flashed before her closed eyes—impressions that she'd long come to associate with precognitive awareness of the future.

She was frightened by what was happening.

She knew that she should run crying for Lizzie, who'd pray for her and with her as she had in the past and would send someone running for Pastor Edgerton.

Lolly knew what was happening.

She knew what she should do.

But her body was so, so weak . . . and her will was ebbing fast . . . until soon she had none and didn't even consider what she needed to do to keep herself safe in the Lord. But the exhaustion, the horrendous exhaustion, was all-encompassing and unrelenting. Lolly was too tired to pray, too fatigued to think, too weary to consider anything but the desperate bodily need to give in and drift off to sleep.

Rest—she needed just a little bit of rest. At that moment, she sympathized with the apostles who'd been unable to stay awake and pray in the garden when Christ had asked it of them. But with only a minute or two of sleep, surely she would be rejuvenated enough to muster strength, conceive of prayerful words that needed to be said, and take action.

But first . . . just a bit of mind-blotting, soul-absorbing, body-escaping rest. . . . Only a moment or two. . . .

And then, for the remainder of that day and part of the next, Lolly slept deeply, as one who had died.

chapter
14

BILLY LeFAVE NODDED thanks as Lizzie poured an after-breakfast cup of coffee for him and Brad.

"Thanks, Ma. I'll enjoy this cup, and then I'd better hit the trail for the lake."

"Is Serenity going to visit her people?" Lizzie inquired.

"I don't know. I figured you'd tell *me* if she was going to ride along. Hasn't she told you?"

"No," Lizzie said. "I figured you'd know."

"She hasn't said a word to me."

"Nor to me."

Billy shrugged. "Then she must not have plans to go visiting for a few days this time."

"Must be she has plans here in town," Lizzie said.

"Or is counting on there being some with a certain lumberjack?" Billy mused.

"What do you mean by that?"

"C'mon, Ma, anyone can see that Serenity's interested in Sven Larsen."

" . . . Is she?" Lizzie questioned.

"Ain't she?!" Billy responded.

Lizzie chuckled. "The way you're carrying on, Will LeFave, I'd almost think that whether she is or not means something to you!"

173

The attractive Frenchman flushed.

"Well, of course it means something to me. I care about the girl, for heaven's sake! She's like a sister to me! And I don't want anyone doing her wrong."

"Sven's a good man. . . ."

"I know that!" Billy said curtly. "But—"

"But what?"

"Anyone harms so much as a hair on Serenity's head—believe me—they'll answer to me!"

"Does Serenity know that?" Brad asked, winking at Lizzie so that Billy missed it and then favoring his son-in-law with a benign and innocent look.

"She should!" Billy flared.

"Haven't told her, have you, Son?" Lizzie inquired.

"Well . . . no. . . . I shouldn't have to. She should just know. . . ."

"Assumptions can be dangerous, Will," Lizzie said. "We can all end up assumin' entirely the wrong thing and takin' action accordingly."

"What are you drivin' at, Ma?" Billy asked, his tone weak and almost strangled, as if he were not quite sure he wanted to hear her answer.

"That Serenity loves you!. . ."

There! The words were finally out!

"Bu—but . . . she's been keeping company with Sven!" Billy pointed out.

Even Brad could see that this fact had pained Billy more than just a little. "She's keepin' company with Sven, Will, only because she's given up on you. . . ."

"Given up on me?"

"Sven's her friend, but 'tis you she loves. Although there's potential for her to really learn to love Sven, if that's what's meant to be. . . ."

Billy made no response, and Brad and Lizzie ceased their intimate conversation with their son-in-law when they heard slow and careful steps descending the staircase.

"Well, well!" Lizzie cried out when she saw Lolly. She went to give the sloe-eyed girl a hug. "If it ain't sleepyhead!"

"Good mornin', Lolly," Brad said.

Billy gave her a curt nod and seemed to stare—almost glare—into his coffee cup.

"Feelin' better this mornin', Lolly?" Lizzie asked.

" . . . I think so. I really slept hard last night . . . but dreamed a lot, so in some ways I'm still tired."

"Rest iffen you want."

"I think I'd feel better if I was up and active," Lolly said.

"Sit down and have some breakfast," Lizzie invited.

"Anything you need help with, Lizzie?" Lolly inquired.

"If you're serious about workin' so's you feel revived through the activity, you could give the room you used to stay in a good cleanin' and dustin'. Ain't had no one stayin' in those quarters for a while, 'n the way train travel's been through this town, we're needin' to press that room into service again."

"I'll be glad to," Lolly said, even though in her heart she had fear and trepidation over reentering the sunny room that for so many weeks had been a place of darkness for her.

She knew that if she uttered a word about her feelings, Lizzie would quickly change her mind, not wanting Lolly to do something she was uncomfortable with and felt vulnerable doing. But at that moment, Lolly felt like a millstone around all of their necks. She felt guilty over all of the work and worry they'd endured on her behalf, and she didn't want to add to the burden by seeming silly in her fears.

It was just a room, after all.

She'd entered it often. This would just be one more time. The last time, she'd been accompanied by a gaggle of strong, fervently praying Christians. Now she would do it herself, alone. . . .

And as she made up her mind to do it, she didn't even think to pray that she would be protected in the Lord. It was just one more room in the massive Grant Hotel, that's all. A place where she had once laid her head, as she now did in smaller, cheaper quarters . . . so cozy and safe.

Serenity was one who, like Joy, could slip quietly around the hotel, unobserved. Billy, with his years in the wilds, had perfected the same abilities.

He slipped up behind Serenity. She let out a faint gasp of alarm when he captured her from behind in a gentle embrace but then pivoted her around to face him.

In her dark doe-eyes, he saw expressions flitting and fleeting, even though her features remained basically unreadable.

What he saw was delight—and raw fear—mixed with . . . *undying love?*

"Have you been avoiding me?" Billy quietly questioned.

Serenity only stared at him.

"I take that back," Billy clarified. "It's not even a question. You *have* been avoiding me, Serenity. I want to know *why*. What have I done? I have to know—I wouldn't want some action on my part to forever destroy what we've been through together, have learned because of it, and the Christian love that I believed we shared."

Serenity looked into his eyes, understood all that was contained there, and she knew that the moment ordained for her by the Lord when he laid the foundation of the universe had arrived.

She'd heard Brad and Lizzie talk about Miss Lolly having to "get the offal out of her life 'n keep it out, too!" Serenity understood that, for they kept their Indian camps clean for just that very reason. It hurt to dwell on it, but she realized she had some waste areas in her life that needed to be purged by way of honesty.

Serenity nervously wet her lips. "Not what you have done, William. What Serenity has done. . . ."

"You?!" he whispered, shocked. He couldn't think of anything that she'd done, for he knew that the girl lived an exemplary life and was of value to the people of Williams and adored by her tribe, where already she was doing great ministry work to spread the Gospel and belief and acceptance of Jesus Christ to the Chippewa. "What have you done? What could you possibly have—" Billy sputtered.

Serenity's back stiffened, her tiny form growing a bit taller in the face of Billy's stature.

"It my fault Harmony die."

Tears pooled in Serenity's eyes as she stared up at him, and Billy looked dumbfounded, as if he couldn't comprehend, let alone believe, what she'd just said.

Serenity took his silence as submission to the revelation.

"I killed Harmony," she flatly admitted.

"You did not!" Billy said. "She died a tragic death, to be sure, from diphtheria, but it was a natural death. In these parts—those things simply happen."

Serenity shook her head. "No. My fault. You gave my father, the chief, orders. Nurse Woman not to be bothered—"

"Yes, I know—"

"I knew of order . . . and I defied. . . ."

177

With that, Serenity began to softly cry as she choked out her confession, that one of her childhood girlfriends, whom she loved like a sister, had given birth to an infant, husky, cuddly, cute, the baby almost as loved by Serenity as it was by its mother. "Couldn't bear papoose die!" Serenity said. "I tried. Not work. I had faith in Nurse Woman, so defied your order to chief—and took baby to Nurse Woman against your will. Baby died. Harmony die, too. My fault. . . ."

For a moment Billy was left speechless.

Serenity didn't know what to expect upon her confession, but it mattered not, for she'd commended the situation into the Lord's sovereign hands.

Helplessly, his heart breaking over the torturous guilt that had eaten away at Serenity, Billy put his arms around her, wishing to ease some of her grief and hurt onto himself so it would lessen her intense anguish.

He realized how at one time, had he known, he could have blamed Serenity and grown bitter, believing that she'd caused the departure of his beloved. But now, with time and Christian maturity, he knew that wasn't true. There was a season for all things, and God had a plan for mankind, and Harmony had been brought into his life to work a miracle . . . and now God had given him another Christian woman to edify him as a believing man.

"Shhhh . . . shhhh. . . . Stop blaming yourself, darlin'," Billy crooned. "I don't blame you. Things happen. All things— even tragic events—work for good for those who love the Lord."

"You no blame me?" Serenity said, beseechingly looking up into his eyes.

Billy was helpless not to stare into her beautiful, serene, absorbing gaze. "I'm not blaming you, sweetheart. Won't.

Can't. 'Cause I realize that all along I've been too busy loving you for it to have mattered even if I'd known. . . ."

Thirty minutes later Serenity returned to the kitchen area, her cheeks a deeper rose color, flushed with excitement. She was short of breath.

She asked Lizzie if it would be possible for her to have a few days off to spend with her people at the lake.

"Go ahead, darlin', we'll manage somehow. Lolly seems to be wantin' to help out a tad more."

"You sure?" Serenity inquired.

It was clear to Lizzie that the girl would abandon her desired plans to travel to the lake with Billy and visit her people, if she sensed she was terribly inconveniencing Lizzie.

"You go on along," Lizzie assured, "'n give the chief my respect and affections."

"I do!" Serenity promised.

"Bring him to town with y'all one of these fine days!" Lizzie suggested. "Let us return the hospitality that the tribe's shown to us."

"I tell him!" Serenity promised.

Serenity rushed off to pack a few things, and then Billy came into the kitchen.

"Stealing away the hotel help, are you, Bill?" Brad teased.

Billy flushed but didn't deny it. "Reckon I am. It'll only be for a few days. Serenity's wantin' to be here for Joy's birthin'. And I'd like to be nearby to greet my new niece or nephew, too."

"We won't have many more days to wait now afore we'll know iffen we're bein' blessed with a new boy or girl to add to the family's lineage."

A short while later Serenity reappeared downstairs.

Lolly was staring at the Indian girl as if in a trance. Billy picked up Serenity's small valise, then touched her elbow to guide her toward the door.

On impulse, Serenity returned, gave Lizzie a hug, gave Brad one, too, then even faced Lolly, whom she'd tended to ignore and avoid . . . and touched the gypsy girl's shoulder.

"Good-bye, Lolly. . . ."

The gypsy girl who'd never apologized to the Chippewa maiden and sought forgiveness seemed to flinch from Serenity's touch when she detected that the girl had love and forgiveness for her and was at that moment happier than she had ever been before. Lolly dully nodded.

"Got a hug for me, Ma?" Billy inquired, chuckling as he juggled Serenity's valise.

"You should know that 'thout askin'!" Lizzie said. "Course I do! A bushel 'n a peck's worth!"

Billy shook hands with Brad, collected Serenity, and they were gone.

"I'll go attend to my old room," Lolly quietly said, turning away hesitantly, as if she longed to stay. But she seemed mercilessly and relentlessly driven away, although the others, in their joy, were blind to her misery and confusion.

"Appreciate it, darlin'!" Lizzie said.

Then she and Brad were back in conversation as Lizzie did dishes and Brad dried, so they hardly were aware that Lolly Ravachek had just left them. . . .

Lolly's mind was occupied with deep thought, and her limbs moved instinctively as she collected cleaning supplies, cloths, and made her way up the staircase to her old quarters, almost as if it required no will of her own to accomplish.

For a moment, she snapped from the strange reverie as she stood outside the closed door. She regarded it, envisioned the sunny room on the other side, a room that was not dangerous nor foreboding—just another room—and then willed herself to enter.

Lolly chided herself that it was silly to simply fear being in her old quarters, and it seemed such a trifling, inane fear that she did not stop to consider that she should pray for strength and protection.

The hinges whined and eerily creaked, the sound of true loneliness, as she twisted the rattly knob and the door gave.

Sunlight slashed across the room, brightening the center of the braid rug near the bed. There was a light sift of dust on the bureau, which stood with one drawer out of alignment, and on the windows, the floor. The casements of the windows were closed, causing the room to feel almost unbearably stuffy.

The room, which had so long been Lolly's, now seemed that of a stranger, and that awareness was a relief to her. She was not who she was when she'd resided in that room.

. . . Or was she? Deep down in some dark, dank area of her soul?. . .

The horrible and haunting thought penetrated her mind.

I'm not! a part of her protested.

You still are! a taunting portion of her seemed to cry out in a sneering hiss.

I've turned away! the internal argument in her mind waged.

Have you? Have you really? Then what about—

It was as if a committee were meeting in her head, no one paying attention to Roberts' Rules of Order as back and forth the arguments raged, with Lolly feeling as if she were being cut to shreds by a shrewd, merciless, accusing prosecuting attorney, while her own defenses seemed weak and stuttering.

If only I knew what to do, Lolly thought, her face plaintive as she set about to dust and clean the quarters for future guests to inhabit.

There was so much to think about.

She considered the way poor Serenity had patted her shoulder — and the jolting psychometric sensation and strange knowledge that had seemed to sear into her mind at the touch.

Lolly felt pain and guilt when she considered how she'd threatened Serenity, promising to reveal her worst secrets if Serenity didn't do her bidding.

As a newborn Christian, she hadn't taken the time, nor faced the opportunities presented, to apologize to Serenity, wish her well, and assure her that she would do and say nothing to cause Serenity's peaceful life to become a nightmare before her eyes.

It was a door left open. . . .

And William! She'd so long believed he was hers that even after she'd turned away from the occult, she'd continued to believe in her heart of hearts that he *was* the man destined for her, and the idea of giving up that belief pained her to the core. She'd clung to the conviction that one day he would be hers. She hadn't fully trusted in the Lord—she'd counted on the forthcoming reality as revealed by the cards and ball. But Billy was so handsome, so wonderful, it would have been a horrendous agony to cast aside the beguiling dream that had comforted her so many times in a new town, among strangers who'd become her friends.

Had it been another tempting doorway to the past left open?. . .

What if the crystal ball was wrong? And what if the Lord didn't intend William for her?

What was she to do with her life?

Where would she go?

She couldn't stand the thought! She felt that she'd sooner be dead. . . .

If only she had some idea of what lay in store for her. If only she knew the peace that until so recently had been hers. If only she could once again manage to pick up the Bible and discover such meaning and comfort from it, as she had in days gone by.

For two days now her Bible had remained unopened. She couldn't will herself to even reach for it. And when she considered devouring Scripture by a force of will, it seemed that such dark and diabolical weariness overwhelmed her that she was simply too tired to take the action that her soul cried out for.

Lolly felt almost dizzy with the strain of her thoughts and the exertion of cleaning the room that was sunny, bright—but stuffy, even with the windows open. It seemed to close in on her.

She felt a need to hurry back downstairs to be with Lizzie and Brad, maybe even take a walk outside in the fresh air to clear her head and go see Lydia and Pastor Edgerton. . . .

"I'll do something," she quietly promised herself as, with dust cloth and cleaning supplies in hand, she stopped to view the perfection of the freshly neatened quarters.

The dresser drawer that was askew marred the effect of the entire room.

Lolly crossed the room, withdrew the door, pushed it solidly in, but it stuck again and would move no further.

Realizing that something was lodged behind it, perhaps a missing sock or a hanky left behind by some long-forgotten overnight traveler, she pulled out the drawer, then knelt on the braid rug to peer into the cavern she'd created.

Blindly she reached in, patted around, and her fingers collided with something solid affixed with a rubber band. Slowly she withdrew it, saw what it was, let out a muffled scream—just as the grandfather clock in the lobby bonged three times, concealing her shriek of dismay.

Then she dropped the loathsome discovery.

For long moments, she stared at the tarot cards lying on the braid rug—and she was in torment as she hung as if suspended while the arguments in her mind raged. Lolly felt weak and vulnerable as the bright room seemed to darken around her and the fresh, pine-scented air wafted in like waves of heat from a furnace intent on consuming her.

Her mind had been so joyously chaotic the day after she'd been confronted and shown the error of her ways. She'd been prayed over, encouraged, scripturally advised, and had come to know the revelations of Scripture as the Word of God, and had accepted his promises as she had accepted Christ into her life.

Pastor Edgerton had warned her that it was a wise and wonderful choice, that she would have the Lord's protection, but that she would have to seek it, and she—more so than many other people from backgrounds milder than her own odd upbringing—would have to ward off evil in his name . . . and resist the dark spirits so that instead of pursuing her, they would flee from her.

In clearing out her occultic clutter and then not stepping foot in her old room again until that very moment, she had not realized that not everything had been destroyed!

Her personal deck of tarot cards, laid aside in favor of her grandmother's deck, had remained behind—almost as if playing a dark and terrible trick on her to tempt her in her moment of confusion, when the desire to know her future so she could face and deal with it had never been more acute, nor the idea more comforting.

They'll never know . . ., the stealthy, secretive idea filled her mind when she thought of her Christian friends congregated in the kitchen down below.

Resist the Devil—and he will flee from you, the correction flowed into her thoughts . . . even as her hand reached out, as if driven by a strange will of its own, to scoop up the tarot cards, grown soft and silken from years of use.

Just once . . ., the thought softly slithered through her mind, coiling in a dark corner. *They'll never know. But you'll know. You'll know if William is yours . . . or if he belongs to Serenity. . . . You'll know if Joy is going to have a boy or a girl. . . . You'll know all the secrets you've longed to discover. . . . You'll know if Lizzie's son is dead or alive. Lizzie! Think of how comforted Lizzie would be if you could assure her that her son was alive and well . . . and even tell her where he was. . . .*

The old ways called hard and horribly to Lolly.

And the faint call from her soul to repent and resist seemed to grow fainter and fainter as she fingered the tarot cards, so well aware of the dark powers and ancient wisdoms that were poised, waiting, to return through the doorway that remained ajar, unsealed, unsanctified. . . .

"Just once. . . . I'll just do it this once . . . then never, never, never again!" Lolly whispered to herself as she began to shuffle the cards.

The oppressive atmosphere in the room seemed to lift, which eased her mind, and with the door solidly closed and sunlight streaming into the cozy room, she began to lay the cards out on the bright braid rug.

She bit her lip in consternation, suddenly wishing that she had not begun to deal out the tarot cards, but she was helpless to abandon them, it seemed, and scrape them into a pile for destruction and renunciation.

Things had already been revealed to her.

She had to know more!

MORE!

Everything. . . . As much as possible. . . .

The future was hers to know—that she might face what was ahead and bear it better than she might if the future was to come upon her one day at a time, surprising her with what life contained for her and those that she cared about.

"No!" she cried out when the cards revealed that Joy Childers was going to die in childbirth and that her deformed baby would, too. Lester, in his grief, would become a hard-drinking man and die an alcoholic ne'er-do-well. "Please, no!"

But it was in the cards.

And Lizzie—vibrant, bright, vital Lizzie—would end up a helpless cripple in a wheelchair and become a bitter woman with a sour attitude, a bane instead of a blessing to those who knew her. And Brad was going to die a horrible and wretched death, as had all of Lizzie's beloved husbands.

"Please—don't do that to Lizzie!"

She looked for the ones about Serenity. She saw happiness everywhere. She *was* with Billy LeFave, and their children were beautiful and bountiful, and they lived in a lush mansion overlooking the lake, a property different from where they'd begun their lives together, with a majestic steamship moored in the background.

And a strange but handsome fellow was as involved in the business as Billy. A partner!

Who was he? Lolly didn't know, and she muttered curses at the cards that they were deceitfully withholding wisdom from her.

Lolly's eyes went back to the card representing Serenity. Such joy in her future, such contentment. . . .

When Lolly saw what Serenity had attained as being somehow stolen from her after having been promised her by the crystal ball, the knowledge caused a dark part of Lolly to grow livid. At that moment, she despised Serenity and her happiness the way she had never hated anyone or anything in her life—not even Aunt Zita. She despised them all. She was going to leave Williams and its boring town of do-gooders!

Forever!

But first . . .

Lolly shuffled the cards, dealt out with herself the "fool," and she despised what she saw.

Happiness for Serenity—and only misery, rejection, destruction, and death for herself.

Witch . . . witch! the judgment came screaming back into her mind to further deject her. *Suffer not to let a witch live!*

As one possessed, she quietly spirited to her new quarters, the tarot cards tucked within the basque of her dress. She jerked a quilt from the bed, rolled it up snugly around her few possessions, and jammed them to bulging into her valise.

Stealthily slipping down the back way, she stole out the rear entrance. Her valise gaped open with the bulk of the purloined quilt from the Grant Hotel.

Lolly was sidling by the shed and toward the side yard when she heard a door bang. She leaped into the shed, heart pounding, and stayed there until it was safe.

She moved toward the door of the shed and almost screamed when a dusty hank of rope snaked across her face. She jerked it in alarm, the loose knot over the rafter fell slack, and the rope slithered around Lolly. She was about to cast it aside, then realized she could use it to secure her quilt and form a bedroll.

She would spend at least that very night out in the woods, safe under bushes in a thicket patch, until she—and her grandmother's cards—could decide what to do next. . . .

It was in the cards that she would die—but until then she was going to live it up! And trust the cards to guide her on her way.

Lolly headed out of town, not paying attention to what direction she went. Soon she was in the deep woods, aware that she seemed to be traveling in circles as she battled her way through the tangled brush.

"Good heavens—she *is* gone!" Lizzie gasped the next morning when she and Brad, alarmed over the fact that no one had seen Lolly, went in search of her and, getting no answer from knocks on her door, ventured quietly into the room to reassure themselves that she was all right.

"Clearly she is," Brad said, looking around with amazed confusion on his face.

"Wonder where she went to?" Lizzie said.

"Lord knows—"

"And *why?*" Lizzie mused.

Lizzie drifted around the room, softly making an inventory of things that were gone—which Lolly had apparently taken with her.

"It's clear that she went of her own free will," Brad said. "With her possessions gone along with her."

"That's true," Lizzie said.

"But 'tis a small comfort, ain't it?"

"Yes," Lizzie sighed. "Reckon I feel hurt, I do. I got plumb fond of the girl after her deliverance. She got to be . . . like fam'bly."

Brad put his arm around his wife. "She's still fam'bly, darlin', even iffen we never see her in this world again, for she's our sister in Christ. And someday we'll meet again."

"That's a comfortin' thought."

Slowly the pair went downstairs.

"Lolly's gone," Brad broke the news to Lester and Joy.

For a moment they were all silent.

Suddenly Lizzie felt the winds of inspiration sweeping through her, and she knew that she must yield to that unseen force.

"We're Lolly's real fam'bly," she said, "'n right this very instant I think we should all join hands and offer heartfelt prayers on her behalf."

"Good idea, Mama!" Brad extended both hands, which were accepted by others as the family huddled together in hope and belief and petitioned the Lord to keep Lolly safe in his love, to cover her with his precious blood, and to keep her away from the snares of the Evil One.

She tripped over a root that snaked across the ground, and fell hard, crying with the effort. A humming mosquito, then another, hovered in, biting, stinging.

"I'm lost," she whimpered. Then she began to sob. "I'm lost for good. . . ."

The cards can tell you which direction to go.

The defiant thought urged her to action.

Drying her eyes, she reached for her cards, labeled herself the "fool," and began to deal.

They were being obnoxious and malicious . . . for they refused to reveal to her what she desired to know that she might find her way out again and be lost no longer.

As the sun set and the swarm of mosquitoes became a living blankct surrounding her—with Lizzie's quilt little protection against the horrible insects, which seemed to sense any little tunnels in the blanket's depths and fly through them to find her flesh—Lolly was wild-eyed and insane, not only due to the mosquitoes, which were like searing demons from hell, but due to her own thoughts and visions, from which she was helpless to escape.

The dark forces had returned.

And were much, much worse, far more invasive and terrible than they had ever been before.

Death was in the cards for her.

Sooner rather than later, she decided.

Unmindful of the mosquitoes that continued to torment her, she neatly folded Lizzie's quilt, laid the tarot cards within its center folds, looped the rope over a low-hanging branch, placed a knot around her neck, hugged her way up the rough pine bark, rested on a solid branch, gasping for breath, trying to think—

But it was useless. Closing her eyes, she shoved off the rude bark that had poked through her skirt, and brambles rushed up to greet her as the rope abruptly halted her downward momentum and left her feet futilely searching for something solid and eternal upon which she could stand. . . .

Then suddenly the branch creaked, bent beneath its burden, and sank until Lolly's toes touched the good earth.

When she'd faced death square in the eye—and knew that it had been a rash act—in her instant of pain and suffocation she realized how desperately she wanted to live! Jesus had given her new life, but Satan had unleashed his powers to convince her that it wasn't an existence worth living, and torturous thoughts had persuaded her that death was the answer.

With a final creak, the branch snapped downward where it joined the trunk. Lolly's face was red, and her lungs felt as if they would explode as she picked at the knot around her neck. Her fingertips came away bloody from the harsh rope burn chafed on her delicate neck.

"Thank you, Jesus!" Lolly sobbed over and over, each intake of air causing the rope burn to tingle that much worse, but it was almost a joyful pain to know that she yet lived to feel not only with her senses but with her spirit—God's Spirit within her.

Lolly collapsed to the ground, softly weeping, thinking back over her life, unburdening herself of every dark thing she could remember, aware that the blood of the Lamb had covered everything so that her sins were as snow and were no longer even remembered by the Lord.

Lolly stared at the cards, ripped them to tiny shreds, then, digging with her bare hands, buried them in the deep woods, rebuking their dark force powers and denouncing any occult claims on the life that, in that instant, she knew she had wholly given to her Lord, Savior, and Redeemer. . . .

chapter
15

"AMAZIN' GRACE, HOW sweet the sound . . . ," Brad Mathews heard his wife singing, her heart as lifted in spirit as birds flew high in the sky. Lizzie sometimes denigrated her singing abilities, but what she lacked in talents, Brad knew, she made up for in enthusiasm and conviction, and in his mind the meadowlarks couldn't hold a candle to his Liz singing her praises.

He smiled to himself. Lizzie had been bright and sunny, as always, but what had made his wife plumb euphoric was when they'd received an unexpected but very much appreciated letter from Lolly Ravachek explaining where she'd been and what she'd been up to, although she'd not ventured into exactly why she'd left the area in the way she had. She'd hinted that sometime when she came up for a visit, they might converse about it.

Although they'd all entrusted Lolly to the Lord, it had still edified the entire community to know that she was doing all right and living and thriving as a Christian girl making her way in a large city and finding that people in the metropolitan area had a place in their hearts for her, even though she knew that there'd always be a part of her that would consider Williams, Minnesota, "home"—no matter where her gypsy blood might lead her.

Brad Mathews entered the kitchen through the back door near the pantry, set a bucket of end-of-the-season garden produce on the hardwood floor, then crossed over to his wife, who never looked more beautiful to him than she did with a dusting of powder across her cheek. Bread dough was smooth and supple beneath her strong hands. It'd be light and fully dinner rolls fresh from the oven come noon. Then the smell of warm, fresh bread would even overshadow the sweet aroma of roses that seemed to permeate the entire town from Lizzie's and Miss Molly's rose gardens.

"Ready to take a break, Liz?"

"Just about!" she answered.

"C'mon," he said, removing her hands from the bread dough with gentle, loving force, then whisking a clean cloth over it himself. "You've been workin' too hard."

"It's good for a soul!" she retorted. "Idle hands ain't, y'know. . . ."

"Your hands haven't been idle a moment since Lolly up and fled town as she did, which sorta left us in the lurch and suddenly aware of how much we relied on her to lend a helpin' hand. We've been a wee tad busy."

"But such happy busyness," Lizzie pointed out.

"Heavens, yes!"

"Joy bore that young'un o' hers and Lester's like I wouldn't have believed for a first child. I never saw such a healthy infant in all of my days! Growin' like a weed, that little boy is! I wrote all about it to Lolly. 'Spect when I get a letter back, she'll be pinin' to come see that li'l miracle o' God's creation for herself 'n rock him a spell."

"Becomin' a mama didn't slow Joy down, did it?" Brad remarked.

"Sure didn't! I have to rag at her purty frequently not to

overdo. That's why I try to do it myself—so's Joy cain't do it, 'cause I already have."

"She and Miss Nanette sure hit it off."

"It's meant a lot to me to meet the fine woman that Thad fell in love with. Comforts me in a special way that I can't quite give word to. Makes it seem more like Thad's still alive, havin' someone who wants to hear my shared memories of times with that boy as I treasure what she can offer in return."

"Folks in town sure like her."

"Her solos at church services have been a blessin' to us all."

"She's a gracious girl, that's for sure. I could tell she wanted to stay on with us—but when she got the callin' to travel around in these rugged parts and share her godly gift with congregations pastored by preachers that Pastor Edgerton's come to be acquainted with, she didn't hesitate a'tall to answer the need."

"She'll be back any day now on the eastbound evenin' train."

At the mention of a train, Brad cocked his head, listening.

From the distance, off toward Cedar Spur, he heard the faint *whoo-whoo!* of the approaching morning train coming from the east.

"Train'll be here right on time," he said.

He and Lizzie had been placidly swinging on the porch swing on the veranda of the Grant Hotel. Brad stuck out his foot and braked the swing to a halt, then arose, offering his beloved a hand up.

"Let's go meet the mornin' train!" he suggested.

Lizzie gave him a startled stare. "Aren't you bein' a mite bit impulsive?" she questioned. "What's come over you?"

"Don't rightly know," Brad said. Then he smiled. "I just felt such a strong spirit to go meet the train that I'm going to follow that nudging."

Lizzie regarded him carefully, refusing to move until she too felt moved to arise and depart for the nearby depot.

"What were you doin', darlin'?" Brad said. "Testin' the spirits?"

"And what if I was?"

"It's a wise, wise way to live," was all that Brad said as his hand sought Lizzie's.

"The Holy Spirit, the way I see it, he's a gentleman, lovingly guidin' 'n coaxin' 'n nudgin' you to do what he'd prefer for you to do. And . . ."

"And?"

"And the counterfeit, unholy spirit . . . he's a rake 'n a rapscallion 'n a wretch, and he nags 'n threatens 'n accuses 'n . . ."

"We've learned a lot in this little town, ain't we?" Brad murmured.

"And we've been happy here," Lizzie said. "Right now I'm happier than I've ever been in my life. Content as can be. Why, I don't know what it'd take to make me feel even happier—"

"Trust the Lord, Liz darlin', that iffen there's somethin' you need 'n ain't thought of, the Good Lord'll give it to you, iffen it suits his purpose. . . ."

Cedar Spur

Thad Childers was tired, but he was too keyed up to even consider sleep now that he was nearing Williams, Minnesota. He was traveling light, for he had few possessions in life. He had little more than the clothes on his back, his hefty earnings from working aboard the barge in his pocket, and his Good Book, already showing signs of usage, clutched in his hand.

When the train rumbled through Cedar Spur and Thad realized Williams was next on the stop, he felt a surge of anxiety spill over him.

Time and time again in recent days, he'd read the story of the Prodigal Son and taken heart from it.

At that moment, he knew himself to be very much the Prodigal Son. He prayed that his fate would equal that of the returning son whose story had been recorded in scriptural history.

No doubt he'd simply show up to surprise his family.

He hadn't let them know that he was coming, perhaps over the same insecurities the son from biblical times had experienced, and he felt a minor disappointment in his realization that there'd be no parent to greet him at the train station the way the son in Scripture had seen his father recognize him from far off and joyously come forward to meet him for his last steps home.

With any luck, it wouldn't be too hard to find the Grant Hotel. From his ma's letters, he knew Williams was a small town, but she'd described it as a booming area, so it could've really grown up since he'd last considered the village.

Hopefully, the surprise of seeing him wouldn't be too hard on his ma.

Or Brad.

Or Lester.

Or Harmony.

Or the Wheeler girls if they and their husbands still lived in Williams.

He didn't let himself—couldn't let himself—consider that they might've moved on . . . or worse . . . died. . . .

It was almost a relief when the clattering train began to slow, and the bellow of the horn was so loud that it seemed to almost blow away the scary thoughts that had begun to crowd his mind.

The train's brakes clashing, Thad was thrown ahead in his

seat from the force, and instead of remaining seated, he used the thrust to propel him from his seat. There weren't many aboard, so he wouldn't be viewed as rude and pushy if he was eager to alight from the train.

Taller now than he'd been a year earlier, Thad had to duck beneath the overhead luggage compartment. As he did, his eyes were drawn to the depot and the small knot of people clustered there. Strangers, he realized, but no doubt people who'd know his folks and be able to guide him to where they—

"MAMA!" Thad cried aloud, his voice wailing with shocked delight when he recognized her: older, thinner, but looking wise and serene as always and with even deeper laugh lines around her eyes—lines that his ma refused to refer to as "crow's feet," as he sometimes inelegantly did.

Lizzie cocked her head, thinking she'd heard a child call, even above the train's din. She started to turn, then realized she had no child present, and it was just silliness making her think she recognized a young'un's cry the way it seemed a mama always could pick out her own child's cry from a crowd.

"MAMA!" Thad cried when he hit the platform, a bundle under one arm, his Bible in the other.

Brad turned, saw Thad, and looked as if he'd been poleaxed between the eyes. His complexion drained pale with amazement, as though he'd encountered a ghostly apparition.

Lizzie, seeing her husband's shocked countenance, whirled, and she too saw what he stared at. She too felt as if it were a vision, not to be trusted for fear it would turn out to be a deceptive, cruel lie and not a glorious truth. Her mouth opened, but no sounds came out. She stared, her eyes wide, then let out a wail that didn't end until Thad clasped her in his strong arms, covering her tear-sodden cheeks with kisses, squeezing her like he'd never let go again, and she fleetingly thought that such strong arms, such a tall frame, and such hot tears of joy mingling with her own had to be true. Her own flesh-and-blood son had come back to life after he'd long since been given up for dead.

"It's really, really you—ain't it?" Lizzie sobbed.

"Yes, Mama, it's me!" he blubbered back, hugging her and hugging her, as he had when he was a trusting child and had clung to her skirts.

"I—I'd give you up for dead," Lizzie cried, her voice raw with the horror and pain of remembering it, suddenly aware of the tremendous cross that she'd borne each and every day, which had now been removed from her shoulders.

Thad turned away, unable to bear looking at anyone or anything now except the gently hushing boughs of pine trees as he realized what his actions had cost others. But in his heart, he knew that his folks didn't tote up the painful cost of loving him and that every account had been released, his debts paid.

"Oh . . . Ma . . . I'm so sorry. But I'm here now—I'll make it all up to you. I promise."

"Ain't nothin' for you to make up, Thad," Lizzie said. "Just stay the man you clearly are at this moment. That's good 'nough for me!"

"Son, it's so good to see you," Brad said, shaking Thad's hand, then pulling him into a fatherly embrace, unashamedly mopping his face with his handkerchief.

"It's real good to be here."

Sudden silence that demanded no spoken words engulfed them, and they stood together, huddling in shared hugs, taking in the scents, sounds, and sighs of delight at what it was to be—and be with—*family* again.

Practical Lizzie was quickly back in her long-established role of giver of love and sustenance.

"Hungry, Son?" she instinctively inquired.

"Well, it's been a while since I ate," he said.

"There's fresh sugar cookies at the hotel," Lizzie said. "But mind you that you don't make a pig of yourself, Thad Childers, and spoil your appetite for dinner!" she said then, as she had so many, many times during her boy's years growing up to mature manhood in the Lord.

"Some things never change," Brad said, laughing.

Thad shook his head, hugged Lizzie, and there was fervency in his tone when he said, "Thank the Lord for that!"

"Step lively, young man," Lizzie said, looping her arm through Thad's. "And brace yourself to hear a lot o' news, both good news and sad. But praise God, more blessin's than trials and tribulations. You've got some new kinfolk to meet—"

"Who?" Thad said.

"You never were a patient sort, were you?" Lizzie chided as she steadily continued to dab at tears of joy impossible to stem. But what a pleasure to weep tears of joy instead of sorrow!

"Very well, Ma. I'll wait on introductions 'til you're ready to give them."

"You've got a new brother-in-law, and a sister-in-law who just gave birth to your first nephew!. . ."

"Ma!" Thad cried.

Lizzie steeled herself to break the sad news. "And you've got a sister who's gone on to glory but left behind her husband, who's a brother you'll delight to know."

"Oh . . . Ma. . . ." Almost unbearable pain was acute in Thad's tone as suddenly he realized what his departure from the family circle had cost him.

"Dyin's a part of livin'," Lizzie said.

"Reckon it is," Brad said.

Thad was looking around himself, furtively wiping tears, his chin trembling as he quivered beneath powerful emotions. Brad and Lizzie simply hugged him and gave him the moments to deal with the kaleidoscope of keen and conflicting emotions.

"This appears to be a nice town," he finally offered an assessment. "In fact, it even smells like home. The roses . . ."

"It's home to us now," Lizzie said simply. "And mine and Molly's roses were all started from the bushes on loved ones' graves back in Illinois."

"It's a comfortin' scent to awaken to, and there ain't nothin' like driftin' off to sleep surrounded by the perfume of roses in the night."

"You'll like the folks you'll find in these parts."

"Any nice church-goin' girls near to my age in these parts?"

Lizzie and Brad looked at each other, laughed, then linked hands.

"Some things never change," they agreed, chuckling.

"Well, let me think . . .," Lizzie mused.

"One young lady comes to my mind," Brad said. "I think she'd like Thad."

"Like him?" Lizzie scoffed. "Why, unless I've lost my touch as a matchmaker, she's guaranteed to *love* him! I just know it!"

"What's her name?" Thad inquired.

Lizzie and Brad exchanged a sly glance. Lizzie cleared her throat. "Her name's Nan. . . ."

Thad was helpless not to give a soft, sad sigh. "I knew a Nan once. Wonderful girl."

"Looks like you're destined to meet a Nan again," Brad teased.

"With you two matchmakers in cahoots," Thad accused,

"it's guaranteed to happen. So when do I get to meet this lovely, church-going woman who's likely to be smitten by me?"

"Lord willin', Son," Brad answered, managing to keep his face straight, "she'll be back on the eastbound afternoon train!"

"I guess I can wait," Thad said.

"You'll have to," Lizzie said.

Brad squeezed Lizzie's hand, she winked at him, and they both pictured the tender and romantic reunion, when they'd make a point of seeing Thad to the depot to meet the train from the west with Nanette Kelly as its precious cargo.

"I don't know if I can wait!" Lizzie whispered to Brad. "It'll be such fun to witness!"

"Don't know if I can stand the wait, either," Brad agreed.

Thad, blissfully unaware of the miracle that lay just hours ahead of him, put an arm around each of them, his words parental and authoritative.

"You'll just have to be patient!" he said with more maturity than Lizzie had sometimes believed that boy would ever possess.

Snapping off a rose bloom heavy in its perfection, dew-kissed and sweet with a tangy scent, Thad playfully affixed it on Lizzie's coronet, then kissed her brow.

Her hand squeezed his.

All was forgiven.

The past was forgotten.

A future, whatever the Lord had in store for them, awaited.

"It's good to be . . . home," Thad said as he entered the Grant Hotel.

"Home is where the heart is, ain't it?"

"Let's round up the kinfolk," Brad suggested. "Lester's around here somewhere, Lemont too! And of course your new kinfolk!"

"Ain't got a fatted calf," Lizzie said, teasing Thad as she hugged him close. "But I've got fried chicken, dressin', mashed potatoes, 'n all the trimmin's just like you always loved 'em, my prodigal son."

"It's goin' to be quite a reunion!" Brad predicted as he left his wife and son to their moments of privacy while he set out with the wondrous news.

"Now, there's goin' to be a lot of hubbub this afternoon," Lizzie warned Thad, "when everyone collects to welcome you home. You know how time flies when you're a-havin' fun. So help me to keep an eye on ol' grandfather clock. Leastways the festivities will keep me from countin' every ticktock of the clock as I wait for the arrival of the afternoon train from the west. . . ."

And the love of Thad Childers' life . . .